Four-Legged Suspect
(A Tail Waggin' Mystery)
By Cynthia Hickey

DEDICATION

To all those with a four-legged friend.

Chapter One

Running late, I thundered down the stairs to Tail Waggin' with Sheba so close on my heels she almost knocked me down. The mastiff darted to the front window and stared out.

"That's rude." I glared and booted up my computer.

Sheba glanced over her shoulder at me, then back out the window. When I didn't respond, she turned and stared.

"Give me five minutes, then I'll take you out."

Her big dark eyes stayed glued on me.

"Fine." I'd already taken her out to do her business not an hour ago. But, it looked as if emails and reservations would have to wait. I grabbed her leash, clipped it to her collar, and unlocked the door.

An unearthly howl raised the hair on the back of my neck, and I stumbled back. Once I'd gained control of my senses, I noticed a beagle was tied to the light pole. I glanced around for its owner. Not seeing anyone, and since none of the shops in the strip mall were open, I approached the dog and knelt down. "Did someone dump you off, sweetie? You poor thing." A piece of paper stuck out from under its collar.

I pulled it free and read, "*Barney is a thief. Six months old. Good luck.*" I scrunched up my mouth. "What in the world could a dog possibly steal that would warrant this type of behavior from its owner?"

Barney leaped up and licked my face.

"What's that, Trinity?" Shar, my friend and the shop's dog groomer, arrived for work.

"A beagle." I climbed to my feet. "Someone dumped him off. Called him a thief." I waved the paper in front of her.

"That breed just digs and howls."

"He's cute." I untied him from the post.

"Yeah? Well, so are Honey and Prince, and your parents are still working with a trainer to teach them to behave." She held the door open for me and the dogs to enter. "You need to buy a farm the way you take in animals."

"I'm a pet store. I'll find him a new home." I put the beagle in the dog pen and tossed in a chew toy.

Sheba planted herself next to the pen and rested her head on her paws. Her brow furrowed, no doubt resigned to yet another animal stealing my attention away from me. Not a chance. Nothing could take the place of my big fur baby.

Barney opened and closed his mouth repeatedly causing the toy I'd given him to squeak without ceasing. "I should have given him something quieter."

"I could hear the noise outside," Heather said, setting her purse behind the counter. "He's cute."

"What's making all that racket?" Brad entered, coffees in hand, a tradition he carried on after someone murdered his father. "Oh. A beagle. I've always wanted one."

"You can have him." A pounding started in my temples. "Someone left him outside with a note that said he's a thief. Brad, meet six-month-old Barney."

He set the coffees on the counter, gave me a quick kiss, then picked up the puppy. "Hello. Want to me my fur friend?"

"Definitely need a farm," Shar said. "Between the two of you, you own three cats and two dogs."

Brad laughed. "Maybe I'll buy a hobby farm. How would I look in overalls?"

"Sexy." I chuckled, picturing the image of my wealthy businessman in dirt-covered overalls and tall rubber boots.

"If you get a chance today, call that gal who trained Sheba. I have a feeling my little buddy can use her." Brad set Barney back in the pen.

"I sure will." I agreed. The beagle puppy could definitely use some training, at least for the howling if nothing else. "Want to take the dogs to the lake this evening?"

"Sounds like a date." He came and gave me another kiss, then headed across the parking lot to his office in the theater.

"Why doesn't he have a normal office in a building complex somewhere?" Shar asked.

"He likes the theater." I shrugged. "Says he doesn't need to pay for another office when that one works fine."

After confirming reservations for boarding, I headed to the pens in back to feed and water the animals staying with us. When it was outside play time, I let Barney run with the boarded animals, and cleaned the cages. It would make sense to hire another worker to do this part of the job, but I liked being surrounded by cats and dogs more than I enjoyed people. Also, Heather managed the customers better than I did.

Barney barked and bit at the water spraying from the house while Sheba watched. When the puppy jumped her, she held him to the ground with a massive paw.

"Be nice, girl. He's just a baby. Remember, you were a handful not too long ago." I turned off the water and put everyone back where they belonged. Sheba still got into trouble on occasion.

Brad returned a little after five and purchased everything he'd need for Barney before we headed to the lake. The beagle barked out the window at every car we passed. "He definitely needs training. Hush, boy."

The dog kept barking, bringing back my headache. "Why do people leave me with troublesome pets?"

"Lucky, I guess." Brad pulled into an empty parking spot. "Let's tire him out."

A few other people strolled the path around the

lake. A few picnicked next to the water despite the autumn chill. A couple of men sat in folding chairs. The sun sprinkled the water with diamonds and kissed the top of the trees with gold. The lake had to be one of my favorite places ever, despite Sheba having dug up a dead body a few months ago.

Leashes in one hand, and the other hand entwined in Brad's, I strolled with my knight down the path. "How was work?" I asked.

"Good. I'm going to have to head to New York in a few days to look over some property, but I won't be gone but a day or two."

"Good. I like it when you're here." Funny that I'd once thought him guilty of killing his father. Brad didn't have a bad bone in his body. Instead, he'd updated and renovated the strip mall in order to increase business for all his tenants rather than raise our rents as he'd first intended. He'd then built the theater to make up for the income he lost by not raising rents. A decision he says he's never regretted.

"Was the pet shop busy?"

"Not very. We're out of kittens and puppies to sell. Have a few boarders and our daily daycare animals. I ordered some supplies. It was nice to have a slow day." Without having been involved in a mystery lately, no one came in just to ask questions.

Barney strained against his leash, making himself gag. I shook my head. We should have brought a choke collar.

Brad pulled the leash in so the dog would have to walk closer to his side. "Were you able to schedule a training session?"

"Yes. Next Tuesday at ten."

"Good." Brad stopped and put a hand on the puppy's head. "Settle down, buddy. You're only hurting yourself."

Barney licked his hand, then promptly glanced toward a squirrel. He barked, shrugged out of his collar, and took off after the fluffy red tail.

"Barney!" Brad released my hand and gave chase.

My well-behaved girl and I followed at a slower pace. "Hopefully, Barney's training will be as effective as yours was." How would the dog behave in Brad's penthouse? I had a feeling the puppy would be staying with me at Tail Waggin' every day.

Continuing along the path that circled the lake, I grinned every time Barney's bark or Brad's yell reached me. Yep, it hadn't been too long ago that Sheba acted just as rowdy. "Brad's neighbors won't be happy with his new dog."

Sheba glanced up at me, wagging her tail, as if expressing her agreement. Her ears rose as she returned her attention to the path in front of us.

All barking ceased. I increased my pace fearing something was wrong. Seconds later, Brad called my name, and I changed from a fast walk to a sprint. Thankfully, having joined the gym primarily as a way to keep an eye on suspects, I was now in better shape than a year ago. I reached Brad before I panted like a fat man running after a hot dog. "What is it?" I kept a firm grip on Sheba's leash.

"I can't find him. Barney stopped barking.

That's suspicious, right?" Worry creased Brad's face.

"Could be." Or something far more serious. "Have you tried calling him?"

"Of course. Multiple times."

I released Sheba. "Find that rowdy pup, girl."

Nose to the ground, she took off. Brad and I followed at a run.

An excited bark alerted me to the fact we closed in on our prey. I stopped and studied the area around us. Not a lot of trees, but plenty of people lounged or strolled by the lake. Barney had to be with one of them.

A man's shout rang out above the other voices. I whirled to see Barney, ears flapping, racing toward us. A burly man gave chase.

Barney dropped a watch at Brad's feet.

"Is that a Rolex?" I asked. "A real one?"

"Yep." Brad turned it over in his hands. "There's an inscription. To the only man I'll ever love. Margie."

"Do you think it belongs to him?" I motioned to the man quickly approaching.

"We're about to find out." Brad kept a pleasant expression on his face.

"That your dog?" The red-faced man stopped in front of us. Anger flashed in his eyes.

"Yes, sir." Brad's smile didn't waver.

"He's a menace. Got into our picnic supper and stole my watch." He held out his hand.

"I'm very sorry about that. I just got him today, and he hasn't been trained."

"Ought to take him to the pound. If you can't

control your dog, you shouldn't have one."

Sheba, hackles raised, stepped between me and that man. Trusting my dog's instincts, I figured something wasn't quite right about the guy. "There's an inscription on that watch. What does it say?"

"Mind your own business, nosy woman." His eyes narrowed and he wiggled his fingers for the watch.

Brad placed the watch in his palm.

"I know who you are. You're the pet store owner. The one who sticks her nose where it doesn't belong. Be careful, or you'll stick it somewhere and won't get it back." The stranger turned and marched away.

"That sounded a lot like a threat to me." I glanced at Brad.

"I agree. Makes you wonder whether someone is missing an expensive watch. And not the man I just handed it to."

Chapter Two

I refused to get involved in another mystery, so I threw off my covers the next morning and marched to the shower, chanting, "I will not. I will not."

Was it my fault folks around Waterfall, Arkansas, knew me for solving mysteries? No. I had a knack but came too close to death too many times. No more. I turned on the hot water, then the cold, adjusting the temperature to the way I liked it.

Murder and theft, love triangles…all ruined the picturesque façade that was Waterfall. Working in my pet store, caring for my pets, and loving Brad gave me a full enough life without facing danger. Right?

I stepped under the shower's spray, forcing the cold look in the man's eyes last night from my mind. If I didn't try to find out whether he was the only man Margie loved, I'd remain safe, as would those I cared about. That cemented it. I would stay out of this one.

After I'd showered, dressed, fed the dog and cats, and taken Sheba out to do her business, I left the door of my apartment that led downstairs to the store open so the animals could come and go and headed for my desk. Before I'd booted up my computer, Shar breezed in.

"You're early," I said.

"Lots of grooming appointments today. Since you haven't replaced the van, people have to come to me instead of me going to them."

"I'll ask about the insurance check again." We'd just started our mobile grooming when someone blew up the van, injuring me and Shar in the process. I sent yet another email to my insurance company.

"What did you and Brad do last night?" Shar hung up her sweater. "McIlroy and I stayed in and watched an action movie. I still can't believe it took me almost getting blown up for him to profess his undying love."

I widened my eyes. "He said he loved you?"

"Well, no, but even a blind person could see that he does." She grinned, patted Sheba on the head, and headed to the grooming room.

I agreed, the detective did care for Shar. Still, I hoped she wouldn't get her heart broken. McIlroy seemed very devoted to his job. Had he hired a new law enforcement officer after the last one turned out to be dirty? I shrugged. I'd find out soon enough. News traveled fast in this town.

"Good morning, beautiful." Brad, coffees in hand and Barney on a leash, entered the store and moved right in for a kiss. "I remembered Heather is off today so only brought drinks for you and Shar. Hope you don't mind if I leave Barney with you." He set the pup in the playpen.

"You're wonderful." I'd miss him when he went out of town in the morning. I didn't like needy people, so I refrained from telling him how I hated that he had to go.

His gaze caressed my face. "You didn't dwell too much on the watch last night, did you?"

"Nope. I vowed this morning not to get involved." I sipped my mocha frozen java.

"That's my girl. How about I cook for you tonight?"

"That sounds great."

"Want to stay in the penthouse while I'm gone?"

"Why?" I raised my brows. "I'm not in any trouble. Staying home makes it easier to get to work."

"It's just an offer, sweetheart. If you change your mind, tell the new doorman, Morrison. I'll leave your name with him."

I nodded. "I'll take care of the animals." Guess I'd be taking Barney to training.

"Thanks. See you later." Another lingering kiss and he headed across the parking lot.

"Why don't you move in together?" Shar asked, rejoining me. "You don't have to share a room. He has a guest one."

"I like my independence." Plus, I was an old-fashioned girl. Unless I was in danger, I didn't want to live with a man outside of marriage. Not to mention my mother would have a coronary. Speaking of—

"Hello, dear." Mom breezed in with Honey, her Corgi, trotting beside her on a leash. "Look how well she behaves now. Prince rules the house but isn't the menace he once was. That cat knows who fills his food dish. These two only needed some loving and stability."

Luckily, Mom and Dad were willing to provide those things. After the murder of their previous owner, the two fur rascals had driven me crazy trying to keep them under control. "What are you up to today?"

"After walking this girl, I have a hair appointment. Can I leave her here for now?"

"Sure." The place was filling up quickly with pet daycare clients, and none of my regulars had arrived yet.

By lunchtime, we had a full house. The comings and goings kept Barney hyper and vocal, causing me to place a call to the trainer, Mrs. Bridges. "Please tell me you can squeeze me in."

"I had a cancelation. Can you come now?"

"Absolutely. Shar, mind the store." I clipped a leash on Barney, called for Sheba to follow, and rushed to my SUV. Brad would be so surprised when he came back in a few days to a trained dog. I'd try not to ruin the surprise at supper that evening.

Mrs. Bridges waited near a wooden fence, frowning as Barney set up a frenzied bark fest. "I know just the thing. Follow me."

With Sheba following obediently, I tugged

Barney after the trainer. "You are a handful, mister."

"We'll get him fixed up." Mrs. Bridges stepped into a small metal building and came back out with a black collar in hand. "This is a shock collar. Try to use the high pitch or the vibrate button first. Only use the shock if nothing else works. We don't want a skittish pup." She fastened it around his neck. "Press one of the buttons on the remote when he exhibits undesirable behavior." She handed me the remote.

"Too bad this doesn't work on people."

She laughed. "The ones for larger dogs would be quite effective." She petted Sheba. "This girl didn't need such a thing."

"She's a very good dog. Tolerant of less well-behaved ones." Pride rose in me.

"I'm surprised you bought another dog."

"This rascal belongs to my boyfriend."

"Ah. Well, bring him back if this doesn't work. We can cancel Tuesday's appointment for now."

Feeling optimistic, I headed back to the store with Barney. I was eager to see how the collar would work.

"Great idea." Shar stood from my seat behind the counter and eyed Barney's collar. "I'd like to borrow that when he's finished with it."

"For what?" I frowned.

"To keep McIlroy in check." She laughed and headed back to her grooming.

"I heard the most interesting news at the salon," Mom said from behind me. "There's a new woman in town. Margie Flamell. She's quite the little mouse but interesting."

Margie? I arched a brow. "How so?"

"Richer than Methuselah, if I'm a good judge."

"There are a lot of wealthy people in this state, Mom." I took my place behind the counter.

"Not a lot of them have been burglarized recently though." A secret smile spread across her face. "Margie said someone broke into her house in Silver Brook two nights ago and took quite a bit of jewelry, guns, and electronics. She's beside herself, living alone and all." Mom sat in a chair near the window. "I told her we'd help find the thief."

"You didn't!" There went my resolve not to get involved.

"Well, of course, I did. We're quite the crime-fighting team."

"Did I hear crime fighting?" Shar poked her head around the corner.

"You did." Mom nodded, then explained about the burglary again. "I told Margie we'd be over right after the store closed." She glanced around. "Why not let Heather have weekends off so she could mind the place when we have other work to do?"

"Robbie had a doctor's appointment, so I let her switch days." I rolled my eyes, trying desperately to think of a way out of this. "I'm having supper with Brad tonight."

"What time?" Mom tilted her head.

"Seven, I think."

"Perfect. It won't take long to question Margie." She stood. "See you at five o'clock on the dot."

I preferred it when Mom and Dad were traveling

Europe. When I got into a fix myself. "Fine. But this is not some kind of a club."

"Yes, it is," Shar said. "I've mentioned it before. Now, it's official. The Waterfall Sleuths ride again. We'll take the Thunderbird."

As soon as I locked the door to Tail Waggin' at five o'clock, Shar pulled up in her aqua 1957 Thunderbird convertible. Since Mom already sat shotgun, I climbed in back trying to ignore Sheba's sad gaze through the store's front window.

Twenty minutes later, we pulled in front of a restored Victorian house. I didn't bother asking how my mother knew where Margie Flamell lived. Mom could weasel information from a turnip. "Let's get this over with. Brad is leaving in the morning, and I don't want to be late for supper."

"Where's he going?" Mom asked.

"New York."

"You should go with him."

"I have a business to run."

She shook her head. "I'm capable of running a pet store for a few days."

"No, thank you." No telling what I'd come home to.

Mom rang the doorbell.

A petite woman in her early forties opened the door. For some reason, I'd figured her to be older. Worry creased her pretty face. "Thank you for coming. I've tea on the back porch." I could barely detect a Southern drawl in her soft voice. "There are finger sandwiches, too, if you're hungry."

"We can't stay long." I sent a sharp look to Mom and Shar, making sure they caught my point.

Mom rolled her eyes. "You shouldn't have gone to any trouble."

Once we were seated, Mom pulled a small notepad from her purse. "Why don't you tell us what was taken? My rude daughter wants us to rush, so we might as well get straight to the point."

Margie nodded. "A Rolex I'd bought my husband before his death, my wedding ring, a few less expensive items of jewelry, a laptop, several televisions—"

"Did you call the police?" Shar leaned forward.

"I did, but they didn't seem to think they could retrieve the items easily."

"Did the watch have an inscription?" I locked my gaze on hers.

"Yes. *To the only man I'll ever love. Margie.* How did you know?"

"Did your husband have any relatives he might have given the watch to?"

She shook her head. "It was just the two of us. Why?"

"Because my fiancé and I—well, his dog— found a watch with that inscription by the lake last night. A man came up and claimed it."

"There you go." Mom clapped her hands. "We've already discovered more than the police."

Unfortunately, that meant I was getting involved in another mystery. Brad would wring my neck.

Chapter Three

"You're what?" His fork paused halfway to his mouth. Mashed potatoes plopped to his plate.

"In my defense, Mom and Shar roped me into it." I'd waited until we sat down to eat before spilling the news. I quickly filled him in on the complete conversation with Margie.

He set his fork down, placing it precisely even with his plate. "Why do you insist on these things when I'll be gone?" He sighed. "Solving mysteries is like a chigger under your skin, but when I'm not here, I can't watch over you."

"I promise not to go anywhere unarmed." I smiled. He didn't look angry, but sometimes calm came first. Not that Brad would ever be mean to me. It wasn't in his nature. Instead, the wounded look in his eyes was like a stab to my heart.

"Thank you for taking Barney to the trainer." He picked his fork back up.

"Are you angry?" Tears clogged my throat. "I

17

really did mean it when I said I had no desire for more mysteries."

He reached across the table and took my hand. "I'm not angry. I know how your mother and Shar can be. It's best you're with them. To be the level-headed one. Just try not to get blown up." He grinned.

"That I can promise. To try at least." I leaned over and offered my lips for a kiss. "You're welcome with Barney. I figured he'd be in the store a lot."

He pressed his lips to mine. "I'm sure you'll have him in tip-top shape when I return."

I laughed. "I'm not a miracle worker."

We stayed up late watching a comedy before Brad drove me home. "Please be careful. I'll call you every night."

"I'll do my best. Since all we've done is speak with Margie, there isn't much else unless something happens. I'll talk to McIlroy today, but other than that, I'll be at the store all day."

"Good."

I woke the next morning gritty-eyed from lying in bed wondering far too long what our next step would be. Waterfall Sleuths. Ha. The things Shar came up with.

Mom arrived with Shar as I turned the closed sign to open. "Doughnuts and coffee," she sang and set them on the table near the window. "Since Brad is gone, I'll fill in."

"Doughnut-shop coffee?" I wrinkled my nose.

"It's real coffee. Not the froufrou stuff you drink. I had them put extra cream in yours." She opened the box to reveal twelve beautiful, glazed doughnuts.

"You're forgiven." I took one and bit into sugary heaven.

"Yay." Heather entered and sniffed. "I didn't have time to eat this morning." She made a beeline for the box. "Robbie has an ear infection."

"Poor dear." Mom patted Heather's shoulder. "He'll outgrow them, hopefully. Now, we should formulate a plan to find Margie's thief before the store gets busy."

"I need to check emails and reservations first. I do have a regular job." I licked sugar from my fingers and headed to my desk behind the counter. Normally, I could work in my office, but I preferred being out where the action was.

"Fine. Shar and I can handle this until her first customer arrives." Mom took a seat and pulled a pad of paper and a pencil from her purse.

Leaving them, no doubt, to come up with something ludicrous, I texted McIlroy asking if he had time to meet with me today. He replied that he'd be by in a while. That bit taken care of, I replied to emails, paid some bills, and half listened to Mom and Shar.

"We need a stakeout," Shar said.

"Where?" Mom tapped the pencil against her lips. "Margie has already been cleaned out."

"Her neighborhood. The thief could be canvassing other houses. What did the man by the lake look like, Trinity?"

"Big, bald, muscled, angry." I stared. A stakeout? Really?

"There you go." Shar pointed at the paper. "Write that down. He's our only suspect."

"We don't know that he stole the watch," I said. "He could have bought it from the thief. Don't accuse without evidence."

"Oh, pooh. We'll find the evidence." She waved a dismissive hand, then frowned as Mrs. Nelson entered the store with her schnauzer, Greta. Barney immediately started barking. "My appointment is here." She rose to her feet and took the dog's leash. "Good morning. I'll have her ready by eleven."

"Thank you." Mrs. Nelson's thin lips almost smiled. "I need some more of that dog food she likes and a flea-and-tick pill, please. Can't you shut that dog up?"

"We're working on his training." I pressed a button on the remote on my desk.

Barney's ears went up and the barking ceased.

"I'll fetch those things for you." Heather headed to the supply room in back.

"Your hair looks nice, Mrs. Nelson," Mom said, patting her own new hairdo. "What did you think about Margie's declaration yesterday? We're going to help her find the thief."

I grimaced. The last person Mom needed to tell that information to was Mrs. Nelson. The fact we were getting involved would be all over town within an hour.

"A locksmith is coming over in an hour to put another dead bolt on my doors," she said. "A woman living alone can't be too careful. This town is full of sin and debauchery." She glared at me. "Ever since your daughter opened this shop, we've had nothing but trouble."

Not fair. Trouble started with Brad's father's secrets, which also resulted in his murder. I opened my mouth to protest, but Mom answered instead.

"That is pure coincidence. I ask that you not spread gossip." Her cheeks darkened.

Mrs. Nelson shrugged. "I call things as I see them. Good day, ladies." She waltzed out the door.

Mom glanced my way. "Don't let her bother you. She's a bitter, lonely woman with nothing better to do."

"I won't." My shoulders slumped. It did seem as if she were right, even though I knew the truth. Even small towns held their secrets. I just happened to have a talent for exposing them.

"Your face says you're bothered by her comment."

"Seriously, I'm not." I turned my attention to the parking lot where McIlroy's squad car stopped out front.

"Since no dead bodies have turned up," he said after entering the store, "I have no idea what you want to talk to me about." He glanced through the window behind me and waved at Shar.

"Did a Margie Flamell file a report about a theft recently?" I leaned my elbows on my desk.

Surprise flickered across his face. "Not to my knowledge. Things have been relatively peaceful the last few months."

"She told us she'd been robbed. The beagle there stole a Rolex from a man who claimed the watch was his, but according to Margie, it was one of the stolen items." Why would the woman lie?

"I'll send Officer Rickson over to talk to her. Maybe the report was misplaced before reaching my desk."

"Does that happen often?" I arched a brow.

"Never has before, but if she called it in and our new receptionist took down the information, it's possible. The woman is…not quite qualified."

His way of nicely saying she didn't know how to do her job.

"You aren't getting involved, are you?" He narrowed his eyes. "It never goes well."

"Of course, it does." Mom stepped next to him. "My girl always catches the bad guy. We've offered our services to Margie. As any good neighbor would."

"God help us all." He shook his head. "Don't know what you can do in this case, but make sure to let me know if you get lucky and find out something."

"Don't you want to know what the man with the Rolex looks like?" Mom put her hands on her hips. "Tell him, Trinity."

"Big, bald, muscled, and angry."

"Ever see him before?" McIlroy asked.

"Nope, but I don't know everyone in Waterfall or the surrounding towns. Our lake is a popular place when the weather is nice." I pressed a button on the remote to stop Barney's racket.

"I'll let you know what Rickson finds out." He turned as our delivery man, David, entered.

"Detective?" David greeted McIlroy, but his gaze settled on Heather. The two had been dating for several months now that her divorce from her jailbird husband had finalized.

"Hello." McIlroy headed for the grooming room.

Seeing all the romance in the air made me miss Brad something fierce. I sent him a text letting him know I missed him.

He immediately replied, "I missed you from the moment I dropped you off last night."

The man was too sweet. I smiled and returned to work while Mom huffed and puffed waiting on Shar.

"How long does it take to shampoo a dog?" She frowned to where Shar and the detective talked. "If he'd leave, she could finish."

"It won't take long." I ducked my head to hide a smile. "Why don't you go to the drugstore and buy some new fingernail polish?"

"I don't need any." Her eyes widened. "That's what I used to tell you to get you out of my hair."

I laughed. "You're driving me nuts with all the pacing. What's Dad doing?"

"Piddling in his workshop. I need a bookcase." She plopped back into her chair and drummed her fingers, her nails tapping on the tabletop.

"Mom."

"Oh, fine." She grabbed her purse. "I'll go ask some questions." She marched from the store.

Maybe her leaving alone wasn't a good idea. Too late now. How much trouble could she get into in an hour at the strip mall?

"Stay out of trouble," McIlroy said as he left. He pretty much said the same thing to me every time. It was kind of our thing.

"Where'd Lou go?" Shar led Greta from the grooming room.

"Snooping. She drove me nuts waiting for you."

"She went without me?"

"I'm sure you can catch her." I could use the break without the two of them spouting nonsense.

"Great. My next appointment isn't for another hour." She sped off in search of my mother.

"Clever girl." Heather grinned. "Between those two and Barney, this place is a circus. Think they'll discover anything?"

"Not unless they can find out why Margie lied about calling the police." Which I doubted anyone in the mall would know.

"Embarrassment?" Heather shrugged. "Maybe she's a recluse who is uncomfortable with attention on herself."

"Margie did seem shy, but most people would want their things returned. She told us she had called, and the police told her they didn't think they could retrieve the items."

"Fairly true. Maybe she got that info from TV."

Maybe. I stole a lot of my ideas from true crime shows. I returned to my computer, not worrying too much about Margie's problems. Doubtless, the Waterfall Sleuths could uncover anything of value to the police with so little to go on.

Unless Mom's telling Mrs. Nelson about us snooping drew some bad guy out of the background. I sure hoped not. If nothing surfaced, Mom and Shar might give up, and I could keep my resolve of not getting involved.

Sirens drew my attention to the window. A

police car sped by, lights flashing.

I joined Heather at the window.

Mom and Shar were rushing toward the store. They burst inside.

"Another robbery," Mom said. "This time in Waterfall. We've found us a mystery to solve for sure."

Just great.

Chapter Four

I glanced at Heather. "Do you mind?"

"Not at all. Go. I'll mind the store." She waved me away.

I raced after Mom and Shar to the Thunderbird. Seconds later, we sped after the police car.

Our town didn't have a lot of ritzy homes outside of the luxury apartments Brad owned, but there was one development on top of the mountain. That's where the flashing lights and siren took us.

We stopped behind McIlroy. Behind us, Rickson pulled up. Both officers sent us a glaring look that plainly said to stay back. Why all the enforcement power for a simple theft?

"I bet someone died this time," Shar said. "Come on. We'll skirt around the back."

"Uh." I cast a look to where McIlroy and Rickson entered the house. "It's our necks if we're caught."

"Then, we'd better hurry before the place fills

up with lookie-loos." She shoved open her door, followed by Mom, then me.

At least I wouldn't be alone this time if there was a dead body to be found. My gut clenched. There couldn't be another explanation for a detective and a police officer if it wasn't more than a theft.

Staying low, we hurried around the corner of the house. A dog run of yipping chihuahuas greeted us. Cats roamed the yard, some no more than kittens. Who lived here?

Shar waved us toward a back door. Slowly, she slid the arcadia door open, then put a finger to her lips.

I felt she put too much stock in the fact she dated McIlroy.

"Who is it?" Rickson asked from the next room.

"A Mabel Winston. Widow." McIlroy's tone short and curt. "I'm no ME, but it looks like she struggled and died of blunt force trauma to the head."

Mom gasped and clapped a hand over her mouth.

We tiptoed to peer around the corner.

An overweight woman with gray hair lay sprawled between a floral sofa and a glass-topped coffee table. The old-fashioned, crocheted doilies over everything belied the modern look of the outside of the house. Nothing screamed money here, yet the house had to be over three-thousand square feet. A cat statue lay next to the body, which I suspected was the murder weapon.

A lamp lay shattered. Throw pillows on the

floor. A crack in the coffee table. Good for her. It looked as if Mrs. Winston put up one heck of a fight.

"I bet there's skin under her fingernails," Rickson said. "It's likely the suspect sports some nasty scratches."

McIlroy frowned. "Finding the suspect won't be easy. Hopefully, the crime scene techs will find something to help us." He turned.

We ducked back.

"Get out of here, ladies. This is an active crime scene."

We skedaddled to the back deck.

"We didn't go anywhere close to the body." Mom crossed her arms. "So, we didn't contaminate anything."

"Unless the killer came through the unlocked back door like we did." I leaned against the railing. "That means we've left DNA right along with him or her."

"Don't worry. I'll sweet-talk Alex McIlroy out of a bad mood." Shar grinned. "Speaking of the gorgeous devil."

The detective wasn't smiling when he joined us. "I'm not happy about you being here."

"That's obvious." Shar fiddled with his tie.

He stepped back. "I'm on official business. The three of you need to leave."

"Can't you tell us anything?" She cooed.

"I don't know anything more than what you saw and heard." His jaw tightened as he turned to me. "If you want to be useful, herd up all these animals. Mrs. Winston didn't have family."

28

"Isn't that odd? Neither does Margie. The thief is targeting older, single women with no family."

"We can't say that for certain yet. I knew this woman. She didn't deserve to die this way. The least we can do is make sure her animals find good homes." With that, he turned and strode back inside.

"We need to stake out the lake," Mom said. "Try to find the Rolex guy."

"First we need to take care of these animals." I called Heather and asked her to find someone who could deliver a lot of animal carriers to us. I could try selling the kittens and puppies, but the adult dogs would have to go to the shelter. My store didn't have the room. Whatever money I made from the sale of the babies would be donated to the shelter. I couldn't profit from someone's death.

For the next hour, we herded feral cats that did not want to be caught. We literally tried to herd cats and sported scratches of our own for our efforts. By the time David arrived on his lunch break carrying carriers, sweat poured down my back despite the autumn temperature. Like a good sport, he joined in the herding.

When we'd rounded up the last one, he laughed. "I haven't had this much fun in ages."

"You're nuts." Shar leaned against the house. "I've never worked so hard. Mind helping us get the dogs in crates now and back to the store?"

"Sure, but don't tell anyone I've had live animals in my truck. The delivery company frowns on it." He picked up two carriers in each hand and strode to the front of the house.

"Heather has a good man." I swiped the back of

my hand across my forehead. Today's work was far
from over.

"You won't receive much money for feral
kittens," Shar pointed out. "We need to work on
taming them."

"Have at it." I lifted a carrier in each hand, my
heart breaking at the plaintive meows.

"No, thanks." Shar grabbed two for herself.

Soon, all animals were back at Tail Waggin'
where their protests joined in with Barney's
barking. I needed earplugs.

The first thing I did was call the shelter to send
someone over. The second was to put the puppies in
the pen with Barney and the kittens in cages. Then,
I posted an ad in the local paper and on the store's
website. Exhausted, I collapsed into my chair and
armed the now-romping Barney, clearly in his
element with tiny friends to play with.

I agreed with Mom. We needed to go to the lake
tonight…with Barney. Maybe he'd find the Rolex
man again. A stretch, but the best I could come up
with.

Rickson showed up at the store right at closing
time. "Thought you might want to know what
Margie Flamell said when I asked her about the
theft."

"Of course." I shut off my computer.

"Said she thought she had called us, and when
we didn't respond, figured we couldn't be
bothered."

I frowned. "Sounds like a lame excuse."

"True, but I took her statement. My guess is this
town has a thief preying on old women." He shot a

glance at Shar. "She needs to be careful."

"Watch who you're calling old, Mister!" She planted fists on her hips. "I've had a long day, and I'm not opposed to a fight, officer or not."

His eyes widened. "My apologies." He couldn't leave scary Shar fast enough, poor man.

When Dad found out about our plans for the evening, he insisted on coming with us. We loaded into my SUV along with Sheba and Barney, grabbed burgers and fries, and headed for the lake.

"This is *my* thing, Joe." Mom pouted. "We're the Waterfall Sleuths. You aren't a member."

"Still going to tag along. Brad will have my hide if something happened to Trinity." He popped a fry into his mouth. "Sulk all you want."

"A woman needs something of her own," Shar said, glaring over her shoulder. "Something outside of her husband."

"Lou has plenty." Undeterred, he ate another fry and gave Sheba one.

"Ugh." Mom turned away from him.

I had a strong feeling she wouldn't tell him of any future plans. But, since Brad had installed trackers on all of our phones, Dad would still know her location. I smiled and parked in a spot near the lake away from other cars.

"Now what?" Dad asked. "We question every big bald guy?"

I shrugged. "I'm hoping Barney steals something from him again. If he's our thief…hold on. What if the stolen items are hidden somewhere around the lake? Barney could have dug it up."

"The lake is so crowded," Shar said. "Doesn't

make sense."

"Sure, it does. All these people would trample down any evidence of digging." I shoved my door open. "We need to see if we can find places that would make good hiding places."

"At a slow pace, please." Mom opened her door. "I'm worn out from chasing cats."

"We're simply taking the dogs for a walk." I clipped Sheba's leash to her collar, leaving Barney to Dad. "We'll eat our supper at one of the picnic tables, keeping our eyes out for Rolex Man, then take a stroll."

"Sounds like a good plan," Dad said. His shirt rode up as he climbed from the vehicle.

"You brought your gun?" Mom's brows disappeared into her hairline. "You really think we'll encounter danger?"

"It doesn't hurt to be prepared. I've a license to carry."

"Since when?"

"Since you're at the store all day leaving me to my own devices." He winked and led Barney to a nearby table.

I scanned the people mingling around as I ate my bacon cheeseburger. No sign of Rolex Man, but he could be on the far side of the lake. That's where Brad and I had encountered him.

As for hiding places, the nearby woods provided plenty. Could I risk letting Barney run free? Sheba would come when called, but the puppy wasn't yet trained enough. I didn't feel confident enough to gamble with Brad's dog.

After supper, we headed down the path, Mom

and Shar glancing in each direction so fast I wondered how their heads didn't fall off. Dad and I shared an amused look.

"Not very subtle, are they?" He whispered.

"Not a bit." I kept most of my attention on the dogs. Sheba's ears always rose when she spotted anything of interest. Barney, on the other hand, strained against his leash, barking at everyone we passed. My finger got tired of pressing the vibrate button on the remote, but I couldn't bring myself to shock the poor thing.

"Your mother enjoyed Europe," Dad said, "but helping you solve mysteries has lit a light in her I haven't seen for a long time."

"She feels needed."

He nodded. "It's good to see the two of you spending time together."

Laughing, I watched her and Shar, heads bent in conversation. "The two of them are together more than Mom is with me."

"It's good she has a friend."

"Does that leave you lonely?"

"Heck no. We were together twenty-four-seven on our travels. I have lots of time in my workshop now. I love your mother, but it's good for a couple to spend time on their own interests once in a while."

Brad and I seemed to have too much time apart. His business travels kept him gone longer than I'd like.

For once, Barney fell silent. His tail didn't wag as he stared into a thick stand of trees.

Sheba's posture stiffened, then relaxed as

Margie stepped from the trees.

"Hello. Enjoying your walk?" She smiled and petted the dogs.

"Very much. You?" I tilted my head.

"Oh, yes. I had to…uh…well, the restrooms were too far away." A sheepish look crossed her face. "I'm sorry about lying to you about calling the police. My brain doesn't work as well as it once did."

"That's fine." My time spent visiting friends in the nursing home had shown me the elderly could sometimes forget. But, then again, their minds could be as sharp as a needle at other times. Not that Margie was old, middle-aged. Her attempt to pass as being senile wouldn't work.

Which reminded me it had been a while since I'd visited my old friends. They'd love hugging on the chihuahua pups while I had them.

"I'd best continue with my walk," Margie said. "It's the only exercise I get." She waved and headed in the direction we'd come from.

A few minutes later, Sheba stopped again. This time her rigid posture didn't relax.

Keeping a firm grip on her leash, I let her lead me into the woods, the others close on my heels. We hadn't gone far before I spotted Rolex Man digging at the base of a tree.

Chapter Five

"What are you doing?" Dad ordered.

The man froze, then sneered. "Digging for mushrooms. No law against that, is there?"

"Might be." Dad reached for the gun in his waistband but didn't pull it out.

"Stop it, Joe." Mom slapped his arm, then turned back to Rolex Man. "That's a big hole for mushrooms."

"Mind your own business." He threw the shovel at us, grabbed a black bag from the ground by the tree, and sprinted off.

"Mushrooms, my hiney." Shar frowned at Dad. "Aren't you going to go after him?"

"For what? Digging?"

"Potentially burying stolen goods." She threw her arms up with an exasperated sigh. "Men are hopeless."

Being the only rational one in the group, I snapped a picture of the man before and after he

35

ran. Thankfully, Mom's and Dad's question kept him from noticing. "I have photos for McIlroy. He can take it from here."

"Why spoil the fun?" Shar's glare deepened. "There might be other hiding places around. We should at least look some more before dark."

I shrugged. We had a half an hour before it became too dark to see. Already, most of those strolling around the lake had left. "Twenty minutes. I don't want to be out here with a potential murderer."

"Did anyone notice any scratches on the man?" Mom asked.

We all shook our heads.

"I wasn't close enough." I pulled up the pictures on my phone, hoping to zoom in close enough to see. "Maybe, there on his right hand." I squinted. Could be a scratch. "The police lab might be able to determine more."

"The man lied." Dad paced the area. "Not a sign of mushrooms anywhere."

"Of course, he lied." Mom shook her head. "It was the best he could come up with on short notice. Some people are terrible liars. We should've captured and interrogated him."

I widened my eyes. "Who are you, and what did you do with my mother?"

"I agree with Lou." Shar gave a sharp nod. "Letting him go means someone else might suffer the same fate as Mrs. Winston."

"We'll figure this out." We always do.

Dirt flew and hit me in the face. "Barney!" I pressed the button on the remote from stopping the beagle from tearing up a juniper bush.

The dog refused to obey. Dad yanked on his leash.

Barney kept digging.

"He's after something." I grabbed a stout stick and knelt in the dirt to start digging. Seconds later, I held up a black velvet pouch. Opening it, a gold necklace with a single teardrop diamond winked up at me.

"Told you." Shar high-fived Mom. "I know there are more."

"Not for us to discover." I pushed to my feet and called McIlroy.

"You did what?"

"Took the dogs walking, chased off a suspect, and found a diamond necklace," I repeated. "The only thing we meant to do was walk the dogs."

"Sure. Stay put." Click.

A cool breeze blew as the sun set. I zipped my hoodie and stood behind a large tree to try and block the wind. I'd lied to a police officer. Yes, he knew I hadn't been fully truthful about why we were at the lake, but the fact I lied ate at me like a flesh-eating slug.

When McIlroy arrived, I blurted, "I lied. We were here to find Rolex Man."

Shock, then amusement crossed his features. "I know that."

"Oh, well, I'm sorry I lied."

He laughed and held out his hand. "You took pictures?"

I handed the phone over. He sent the photos to his phone and returned mine. "Necklace?"

"Back in the hole Barney dug."

"I'm thinking the police department could use this pup if he's this good at finding stolen goods." McIlroy bent over the hole and snapped a photo, then opened the bag and snapped another one.

"Margie's or Mrs. Winston's?"

"Possibly Mrs. Winston's, but we don't have a list of what was taken. She can't tell us. I do know it wasn't on the list of missing items from Mrs. Flamell." He turned as Rickson and the crime scene team arrived. "You all are free to go. Be careful, all of you. No one knows better how a simple question asked of the wrong person can put a target on your back." He joined Rickson.

"Coffee and pie anyone?" Mom asked. "I made a fresh cherry pie last night, and it's waiting to be eaten."

Dad put an arm around her shoulders. "Sounds wonderful."

We gathered at Mom's and Dad's house where I stepped on to the porch to call Brad. "Hey."

"Hey, back. How was your day?"

I related the events of the day and night. "McIlroy is impressed with your dog." I smiled.

"Maybe he'll be a good one after all. How's the training?"

"Most of the time he responds to the collar, except when he's digging something up. Then he completely ignores it."

Brad laughed. "A minor thing." A few seconds of silence stretched between us before he spoke again. "Rolex Man will know you're on to him now. Be careful, please."

"How much longer?" A woman asked on his end.

"A minute," he answered.

"Who's that?" I frowned.

"Vivian. You've met her. We saw each other in the restaurant and rather than eat alone, she joined me."

Ah, yes. Brad's beautiful business partner who lived in New York.

"Trinity?"

"I'm here."

"Don't worry, sweetheart. You're the only girl for me. I love you."

"Love you, too." Still, I couldn't help but compare my petite self with unruly curls to the tall, willowy Vivian. "Talk to you tomorrow." I hung up and joined my friends and family inside.

"Everything okay?" Dad glanced up.

"Just fine. He'll be home in a couple of days." I sat at a chair with a slice of pie in front of me, refusing to be jealous or insecure. Life was too short. Either I was good enough for Brad or I wasn't. Oh, please, let me be good enough.

The next morning my day filled with people coming in to purchase puppies and kittens from a murder victim. Why did death draw people? In order to assure the little ones went to good homes, I vetted the prospective buyers with questions.

One man, belly straining his stained tee-shirt, scowled. "What do you mean—what am I going to do with three chihuahuas?"

"I ask questions of everyone wishing to purchase an animal, sir." Something about him

39

seemed off. "I wouldn't want them used in training fighting dogs or used as bait. If you are merely here to ask about Mrs. Winston's murder, I don't know anything other than it was a robbery gone bad."

The man cursed and stormed from the store. I wrote down his name, Roy Jones, and a description to give to McIlroy. I'd learned to trust my instincts a long time ago, and right now they told me this man was involved in dog fighting.

I glanced out the window as he climbed into a beat-up truck. A massive blue pit bull's head hung out the passenger window. Not all pit bulls were mean, but this one looked as if he wanted to eat me. Yep. I'd made the right decision.

"That man scares me," Heather said. "Ever been out to his place on 64? What a dump. Hundreds of empty buckets piled around. Lots of pens. Lots of dogs."

"I've never been, but that's why I didn't sell to him."

"Good thing." Heather smiled as a middle-aged couple entered the store.

They oohed and aahed over the puppies, choosing a female. These two I was happy to sell to. "If you're in the market for an older dog, the shelter has the parents to these."

"We'll check them out," the man said. "Maybe breed for ourselves."

"That's a big responsibility," I said. "I'm sure they've been spayed and neutered by now anyway."

The rest of the day went much the same way. Some buyers, a lot of question seekers. By closing time, I wanted nothing more than to curl up on the couch with my cats and Sheba. Except, I needed to go to Brad's to feed Moses and get Barney's food.

I kept the animals in the apartment, Barney in his crate. He was too young to be allowed free rein. His howls followed me out the door.

At the penthouse, I parked in the garage and took the elevator up. Moses greeted me by wrapping around my legs. "Hello, sweetie. Hungry?" The older male cat lived to eat. He didn't seem to care how much time a human stuck around because he ruled the penthouse.

I fed him and cleaned his litter box before taking another quick glimpse around. Everything seemed fine, so I pulled the door closed after me. In the elevator, I pressed the button for the garage level.

The car slowly descended, suddenly stopping with a violent jerk between the third and fourth floor. When it didn't move after a minute or two, I pressed the help button. Nothing.

I glanced at my cellphone. No service in the elevator. Now what? How long until someone noticed me missing? It couldn't be too long. Folks in the complex would be arriving home from work. Someone would notice the elevator stuck between floors.

After five minutes, the piped-in music increased in volume until I thought my ears would bleed. Surely someone would come now.

The lights went out. Now, I sat in the dark with loud music. Pure torture.

I banged on the door and yelled. "Help! Come on. Somebody has to be out there."

Despite having no cell phone service, I sent a text to McIlroy and held my phone as high as possible, hoping, praying the text would go through. Ugh. My screen went dark. Why hadn't I charged it last night? Because I'd been so tired I forgot.

I slid to the floor. My stomach rumbled. I felt for the bag of Barney's food and laughed. I wasn't that hungry, but I was getting thirsty. After more yelling and banging, I gave up. Eventually, someone would come for me. Choosing to take advantage of the dark, I closed my eyes.

I didn't know how long I'd slept, but when I woke, I started yelling and banging again. My heart almost stopped when someone banged back. "I'm in here!" Duh. Where else would I be?

"It's McIlroy. We'll have you out in a few minutes. Don't move. Don't bang on the door."

Thank you, God. My text must have gone through before my phone died.

Finally, the door opened and light flooded in. I impulsively threw my arms around McIlroy's neck and kissed his cheek. "You're my knight in shining armor tonight."

He stepped back and took my arm. "Come with me."

"Okay." Why the urgency? I reached back and grabbed the bag of dog food. "What's the rush?"

"I received your text. When I couldn't reach you, I called Brad. We feared the worst." He pulled me into an alcove. "Tell me exactly what happened."

"I fed Brad's cat, grabbed the dog food, then headed down in the elevator. It stuck between

42

floors. What's going on?" I searched his worried face.

"You didn't have any trouble going up?"

"No." I crossed my arms. "Answer my question."

"Someone stuck a metal pipe in the elevator to stop it, then put an out-of-order sign on the door. If that pipe had slipped out, the car would have plummeted to the garage floor. You wouldn't have survived. Who did you encounter today?"

"Lots of people. I have puppies for sale." My blood chilled. "Had the pipe moved at all?"

"A little. It slid every time you banged on the door. You only had a few inches between you and death."

I'd only upset one person that day that I knew of. Roy Jones.

Chapter Six

"We aren't even close to making someone mad." Shar shook her head when I told her of the happenings of the night before. "It usually takes at least a week before someone tries to kill you."

"You aren't making me feel any better. The only person I angered yesterday was Roy Jones."

She grabbed her purse. "Let's go. Heather can manage the store."

"No way. I'm not going to confront him. He's huge." I'm sure my face paled to the color of parchment paper.

"Let's just take a look around his property. See what we can find."

I shook my head hard enough to make my neck hurt. "Pit bulls."

"They aren't all mean."

"I bet his are." No way. Nada. Nope.

A few minutes later, despite my better judgment, I followed her to her Thunderbird, leaving Sheba behind. If we were attacked, I didn't want my girl harmed in any way.

"Stop being such a fraidy cat." Shar turned the key in the ignition. "I doubt a three-story fall would have killed you. Maybe crippled you, though."

"Gee, thanks." I buckled my seatbelt, glancing at the front glass window where Sheba stared forlornly at me. Poor girl. I rarely went anywhere without her.

Jones lived down a rutted dirt road several miles from town. Heather hadn't been kidding. Junk and rusty vehicles filled his yard. A chain link fence surrounded the entire place with a big sign saying, *Beware of Dog*. I really did not want to leave the car.

"Looks like a junkyard," Shar said, "but I don't think it is. We'll wander the perimeter, staying on this side of the fence." She parked the car behind thick bushes, which didn't do a lot to hide the bright turquoise color of its body.

"That's the best thing you've said all morning." I pushed open my door, peering around for any signs of a dog outside the fence. Not hearing a bark, I followed Shar away from the car. "What are we looking for?"

"A reason he might want you dead." She frowned at me as if I had short-term memory loss.

"That's a pretty broad reason. All I did was deny him a puppy." Well, I suspected he might fight dogs—pit dog against dog, but I didn't say anything. A gut instinct isn't proof.

The sound of barking increased as we snuck around the perimeter. My eyes widened when we reached the far end. Small cages held dogs of many different breeds, some bearing the scars of battle.

"We have to report this," I whispered.

"Not without more proof." Tears welled in Shar's eyes. "We need to find out where they hold the fights and sneak in."

My stomach dropped. "I can't watch something like that."

"It's the only way to stop him." She backed away from the fence. "I'm sure there's a building close by where the fights are held."

God, help us. Jones would surely kill us if we exposed what we strongly suspected happened here. "There." I pointed to a path heading away from the pens.

Shar, taser in hand, led the way. I wished I hadn't left my bag containing my gun in the car.

Several yards into the woods, we came across another dirt road that led to a barn in better shape than the buildings we'd left. No cars were parked out front. No sounds of dogs came from inside.

Shar peeked in a window. "Bingo."

I joined her. In the dim lighting of the barn, I could make out what looked like a wrestling ring without the mat. "Please, can we go now?"

"How do we find out when the next match is?" She moved around the corner. "Ah." A single sheet of paper fluttered on the door. "Wednesdays at nine. That's today."

Great. I'd spend my afterwork hours in terror of what we'd be witnessing tonight.

Back at the store, I debated calling Brad but decided against it. He'd worry and possibly cut his business trip short. I could tell him day after tomorrow when he returned. If I wasn't dead by then. Nor did I call my mother. Dad would kill me if I involved her in something so dangerous. That left me and Shar. Not much of a relief.

"You're doing what?" Heather hissed, glancing at a customer watching the kittens. "Are you insane?"

"Shar's idea."

"You're going along with it." She lowered her voice. "I've a strong mind to tell McIlroy."

"Don't you dare." Shar clapped her on the shoulder. "We'll call him once we verify what's going on out there. Don't worry. We aren't going to enter the barn."

I sagged with relief. We could look in the window, snap a photo, then skedaddle with Jones none the wiser.

"What happened to you trying to find a thief?" Heather planted her fists on her hips. "Why meddle in something that isn't your business?"

I narrowed my eyes. "You can't be okay with this."

"Of course not, but I don't want my friends involved. Leave it to the police." She stormed to the back of the store.

"Is she going to tattle?" Shar fixed her attention on me.

I shrugged. "Don't know." Although I halfway wanted her to.

"I'll take the calico." The elderly woman who'd been watching the kittens approached the counter. "I lost my Bessie three months ago, and the house isn't the same without a cat."

Grateful for the distraction, I smiled. "I understand. I'd miss my cats terribly." Trashcan and Sharkbait brightened my evenings. At least when I could stay home and curl up on the sofa with them. Something I didn't get to do much lately. I retrieved the kitten, suggested a few items the woman might want to purchase, and held the door open for her as she left with the bundle of joy in her arms.

~

After work, I headed to the penthouse to feed Moses, having the doorman escort me in case the elevator got stuck again. We were up and down without any trouble. Hopefully, the rest of the evening would go as well. In and out with no one the wiser.

I insisted on driving my truck that night, since its dark color would be easier to hide than the vintage Thunderbird. If someone spotted Shar's car, it would be a dead giveaway.

Shar, dressed all in black, eyed Sheba in the backseat. "She's staying in the car, right?"

"Yep. She's coming along as a warning signal. Sheba will let us know if trouble shows up." I shot my friend a sharp glance. "We peek in the window, snap a pic, and leave to call McIlroy. That's it. Understand?

"Yes, and fully agree."

"Uh huh." I'd learned my friend meant well but didn't always do what she promised.

I parked off the dirt road leading to Jones's barn and left the back windows cracked to give Sheba air and the ability to send me a warning. "I'm trusting you to watch my back, girl."

"I have your back." Shar exited the car.

"I'm talking to Sheba." I stuck my handgun in the waistband of my pants.

Shar rolled her eyes. "She's way back here. *I'll* be with you."

Right. I eyed Sheba's leash in the back seat. No, I wouldn't risk her. With a sigh, I followed Shar toward the barn.

At least ten vehicles were parked out front, some expensive, some rundown. I glanced at my watch. Eight thirty. There would probably be more coming.

"We'll hide in the bushes until the fight starts," Shar whispered, motioning to bushes badly needing a trim. "You might want to take photos of these vehicles and any that arrive. Alex can track them down by their license plates."

"Good idea. Might as well stop as many of these idiots as possible." I stepped from hiding, pulled my cap low over my eyes, and started snapping pictures, leaning against a Ford truck as another vehicle pulled in front of the barn.

The driver, a man in his mid-thirties, didn't spare me a glance. I snapped his license plate, not wanting to risk drawing attention to myself by taking a picture of his face. At a few minutes to nine, I rejoined Shar and willed my racing heart to return to normal.

"You make a good spy," she said. "You looked like a teenage boy out there. No one pays attention to kids."

"Brad doesn't think I look like a boy." I glared.

"Well, a very pretty boy." Her teeth flashed in the moonlight.

"Shh." I motioned my head toward the barn.

The lights inside dimmed. Shouts rose. Barking and growls filled the air. Showtime.

We started to step from our hiding place, only to shrink back when a man came out and lit a cigarette. When he finished and returned inside, we crept to the window.

No doubt what was happening inside. A massive pit bull and a German shepherd growled and lunged. My eyes full of tears, I snapped photos, praying the shepherd would put up a good fight. I wanted to pull my gun and shoot those watching such a diabolical act. I'd put a stop to this. Not wanting to see the ending, I shrank back. No animal should be forced to fight for man's entertainment.

"Let's go."

Shar's words sounded as if she forced them through a tortured throat. "Yes, please."

A light shone close to my car. I put out a hand to stop Shar. "Someone's there." My heart leaped into my throat. "Call McIlroy." I pulled my gun and stepped from the foliage.

Glass shattered, spurring me into a run.

"Come on, girl. You'll be perfect." Jones reached through the broken window to unlock the door.

Sheba's teeth latched onto his arm. She shook him like a rag doll.

"Down, girl." I aimed the gun at Jones. "Back away from the car."

He turned, hands over his head, a sneer on his

face. "You won't shoot me, little girl."

"Don't you belong back at the fight?" I would shoot him. All he had to do was make a move.

"Someone told me there was a vehicle out here with a big dog inside. I'm always looking for a big dog."

"You won't get this one. Sit on the ground, hands folded on your head."

He lunged toward me.

Shar leaped from her cover and tased him.

Jones shrieked and fell to the ground.

"Find something to tie him up with," Shar said, opening the back of the SUV. "Alex is on his way. We have to hurry before the others get suspicious and make a run for it." She tossed me a bungee cord. "It'll have to do. I'll tase him again if I have to."

I tied him as tight as I could, then grabbed Sheba's leash and secured his legs. "Watch him, girl."

Sheba jumped from the backseat and focused her dark eyes on him.

When he could move again, he shrank back. "She bit me."

"Don't cause me to sic her on you again. Plus, you owe me a new car window." I kicked his leg, anger rising that he thought he could steal my baby. "You're going to jail, Mr. Jones. Along with all your dirty friends." I kicked his leg again. "Shame on you."

Two police cars pulled behind my car, blocking the road. McIlroy exited one, Rickson the other.

"You ladies okay?" McIlroy asked.

"Right as rain," Shar said. "We've got this one. You might want to round up the others before they figure out what's happening."

"There's a fight going on right now." I met McIlroy's gaze. "Please stop it before one of the dogs is killed."

He nodded and took off at a run, gun drawn, Rickson on his heels.

I stared back down at Jones. "That shepherd had better be okay or I will sic my dog on you."

He shrank back. "It's one of my best fighters. She'll be fine, but no one will want her. She can't be tamed after this." He straightened and laughed. "You won't get away with this, Missy."

I leaned close. "Come and get me."

His response made me want to shoot him. Instead, I turned away and let the tears fall.

Chapter Seven

Swiping the back of my arm across my eyes, I dried my tears and wrapped my arms around Sheba's neck as man after man paraded past us. Every one of them, handcuffed, glared at me and Shar.

"You should all be ashamed of yourself," Shar said, wagging her finger. "What would your mothers say?"

The only man cursing and vowing revenge was Jones. McIlroy put his hand on top of the man's head and put him in the backseat of the squad car. "I think I'll take you in myself." He shut the door and stood in front of me and Shar. "While I appreciate the fact we have now shut down a dog-fighting ring, I am not happy that the two of you came out here—alone—to do this." He crossed his arms. "Do I need to lock you up for your own protection?"

"No, sweetie." Shar batted her eyelashes. "We didn't want to bother you if our hunch was wrong.

Right, Trinity?"

I nodded. "Absolutely. We didn't intend for anyone to see us, but when Jones tried to take Sheba, I lost it."

The detective shook his head. "You two will be the death of me. I'll take your statements in the morning. Come by the station first thing. Now go home."

More than happy to follow his order, I drove us back to the store where Shar retrieved her car. "See you in a few hours."

Shar waved her fingers. "Six hours is plenty of time. It's not even midnight." She climbed in her car and roared away.

Glancing back and forth, I headed up the outside stairs and unlocked my apartment. My cats immediately greeted me. "Hello, my beauties. Let's go to bed."

Despite the stress of the evening, I fell into a dreamless sleep and woke more refreshed than I'd thought possible. Too many late nights would do that to a person.

I lay in bed and thought about how lucky Shar and I had been. Who knew what would've happened to us had we been caught spying? Now, all those men knew our faces. Not a good thought. Still, the only one that concerned me was Jones. Not everyone who attended a dog fight was prone to murder, but the look in that man's eyes could turn someone's blood to ice.

My phone rang. I reached over and snatched it from the nightstand. "Hey, sweetheart."

"Are you crazy?" Brad's voice rose.

"McIlroy called you."

"Texted me, actually. What were you and Shar thinking? Babe, you could have been killed."

"Yet, we brought down a horrible man."

He sighed. "I'll be home tomorrow. Do you think you can stay out of trouble until then? Do I need to hire you a bodyguard?"

"No, I took my gun."

"Great. Is that supposed to make me feel better?"

"If you were here, you would've gone with us."

"Well, yeah, but…"

I closed my eyes. "You're a man and we're women. Is that what you're saying?"

He groaned. "Yeah, and I'm sorry. Please stay out of harm's way until I get home. I love you."

"Love you too." I smiled and hung up. My man still had some work ahead of him to realize that women didn't always need a man to save them.

Mom stood outside the store door when I went downstairs and knocked the moment she spotted me. She motioned for me to unlock the door and rushed inside when I did, slapping a newspaper on the table by the window. "Another burglary last night."

Shar entered before Mom had finished her sentence. "Did you tell Lou what we did last night?"

Mom glanced from her to me. "What?"

Shar explained, embellishing the story a bit, making me out to be a gun-toting hero.

"Without me?" Mom's eyes widened. "I thought we were a team of three."

"Dad would kill me. Let's get back to the B and

E. That's what this group is supposed to be about, right?" Why had neither of them brought coffee? I couldn't deal with them without my morning cup.

"Good morning." Heather breezed in, brews in hand.

"Have I told you lately how much I appreciate you?" I grabbed the one meant for me.

"Not nearly enough." She smiled and handed the others their drinks. "What's up?"

"Another breaking and entering," Mom said, "and these two brought down a dog fighting ring last night without me." She plopped into a chair and tapped the newspaper with her finger. "Guess I'll stick to mundane tasks like this."

"Nothing personal, Mom. I simply protected my hide and yours. Who's the victim?"

"They don't state the name, just that it was a house on Orchard Avenue. We should go look for ourselves. No death this time. Unless you think I'm not capable of asking a few questions." She hitched her chin.

"We can go after we stop at the station to give our statements." I sipped my drink. "Heather—"

"Hold down the fort, I know." She smiled. "Nothing big going on today, right?"

"I have some grooming this afternoon," Shar said, "but nothing until after lunch. Let's get this over with. Alex gave me a stern talking-to after I arrived home last night."

"As he should have," Mom said. "What the two of you did was foolish. Still, I would've liked to have been invited."

"Sorry. Next time." I clipped Sheba's leash on

her, made sure Barney was secure in his pen, and marched out the front door.

"Do we know anything other than the street name?" I asked once we were all in the car.

"I'm sure we'll be able to pick out which house." Mom clicked her seatbelt into place. "Just drive."

"Are you going to sulk all day?"

"Maybe."

Shar laughed from the backseat. "No, you won't. Once we start asking questions, you'll brighten up."

First stop, police station. I parked in front of the single-story red brick building, dreading the Q and A and possible lecture from McIlroy. Inside, the receptionist sent us to a conference room to wait.

"Depending on how long we wait will determine his level of anger," Shar said, sitting in one of the padded chairs.

He must be pretty angry because he didn't join us for half an hour. "Ladies?"

"Detective," we said in unison.

"Didn't expect you, Mrs. Ashford."

"We're on a mission. Pretend I'm not here." She smiled and folded her arms on the table.

He looked as if he wanted to ask about our so-called mission but instead took a seat across from us. "Trinity, tell me everything."

I started with us hiding in the bushes and ended with me holding Jones at gunpoint. "It was pretty straightforward."

"Luckily for the two of you." His face darkened. "How are the dogs?"

"They'll live. The humane society is patching them up and will decide what to do with them." Sadness flickered in his eyes. "I doubt many of them will be put up for adoption. Some haven't known anything but cages and fighting."

I swallowed against the lump in my throat. That meant euthanasia. Another reason to want to strangle Jones. "The men involved?"

"All will pay a fine. Jones will go to jail. He's being held without bond." He stood. "Give my heart a break, please, and stick to your day job." With a nod in Shar's direction, he strode from the room.

Mom rubbed her hands together. "That's that. Let's go since the two of you are still intact."

Shar put her hand over mine. "You can't help those poor animals, but you kept others from suffering the same fate."

I nodded. "That's some consolation."

Next stop, a sprawling ranch house on Orchard Avenue. After spotting a flicker of yellow, I drove up the winding drive flanked by magnolia trees and parked in front of a house with crime scene tape fluttering from the porch and a For Sale sign on the lawn. "If there wasn't a death, why the tape?"

"I don't know, but there's a woman trimming those bushes. I bet she lives here." Mom shoved open her door.

The woman shrieked when Mom tapped her on the shoulder and whirled, the hedge trimmer whirring close to Mom's arm. "Don't sneak up on someone like that." She turned off the trimmer. "If you're selling something, I ain't buying."

"I'm terribly sorry, and we aren't selling

anything unless it's help. Were you the woman robbed last night?"

"Yes." Her eyes narrowed.

"I'm Lou Ashford. This is my daughter, Trinity, and this is Shar Carpenter. We're trying to find out who is stealing from senior single women. May we ask you a few questions?"

"Of course. I'm Mabel Leroy. Come to the veranda. I've tea and cookies." She set the trimmer down and led the way to a large back porch crowded with wicker furniture. "Wait here." Mabel returned a few minutes later with a porcelain teapot, matching cups and saucers, and oatmeal raison cookies. "I don't have many visitors, but I'm prepared when I do." She set the tray on the table. "Now, what would you like to know?" Their hostess tossed a cookie to Sheba. "Maybe I should buy a dog."

"It would have given you a warning." Mom pulled a pad of paper from her purse. "Where were you when the burglary occurred?"

"In bed watching TV." She poured four cups of tea. "At first, I thought the sound I heard came from the television, but when I heard glass shatter, I knew differently. I dug my rifle out from under the bed and crept downstairs, calling out that I had a gun, just in time to see a leg disappear out a side window." She took a cookie from the tray. "I've told the police all this."

"We're helping them," Shar said. "Did the thief take anything?"

"A silverware set I had out to polish. I don't think they had time to take anything else."

"Mind if we take a look outside?" I asked. If the thief went out a window, he might have left prints.

She shrugged. "Suit yourself. I've a prospective buyer showing up later. I need to remove the crime scene tape."

"Without police approval?" I arched a brow.

She laughed. "I put it there to draw attention to the For Sale sign. Worked wonders. Isn't it funny how folks are drawn to scandal?"

"It sure is." I stepped off the porch, taking Sheba with me, and made my way around the house, studying the dirt under the windows.

Sheba nosed around bushes, then gazed up at me.

"What did you find?" I knelt in the dirt and pulled a silver spoon from under a low branch. Further searching didn't reveal anything else the thief had dropped. I continued my search, moving away from the house and down a path that led to a garden I figured was full of roses and other flowers during spring and summer.

The well-groomed lawn led to a tiny pond surrounded by weeping willows. This was a property I'd be proud to call my own and couldn't help but wonder whether I could afford such a place. Probably not.

I continued my hunt for clues, keeping a watchful eye on Sheba who darted here and there, nose to the ground, clearly enjoying the space to run.

There. By the water's edge. I placed my foot next to a man's size twelve with a unique pattern of circles and zigzags on the sole. Find the shoe, find the thief.

Chapter Eight

I called McIlroy. "Didn't anyone check the grounds?"

"We're short-staffed. I sent Rickson." His sigh vibrated the airwaves. "Why don't you enter the police academy? You're worth three of what I have here at the station."

"No thanks." I laughed and hung up, promising to put the spoon in a paper bag to be analyzed for fingerprints other than mine and Mrs. Leroy.

I rejoined the others in the house and told them what I'd found. "Maybe you should stay somewhere else tonight."

Mrs. Leroy shook her head. "I'm not leaving this house unless it's on a gurney or behind a moving van. That scoundrel won't dare return knowing I've got a gun."

Probably not, but what if he did? "We're looking for a big man."

"The glimpse I caught of the leg didn't look big.

More like a small adult or a teenager."

Could there be a thieving ring? It's possible. Perhaps the large shoeprint I found belonged to the leader, and he'd stood outside watching to make sure the smaller man did his job. A definite possibility but still a grasp at straws.

"Let's head back to the store. I hate leaving Heather by herself all the time."

Shar and Mom followed me to the car, Mom climbing in back with Sheba after Shar complained of the dog hair.

"And you're a groomer?" Mom frowned.

"I wear an apron." Shar put on her seatbelt. "I have been thinking about a dog, though. Especially with all these burglaries going on. Mind stopping by the shelter? I want one already trained. I'm too busy to start from scratch."

"Sure." I glanced at her in surprise. "Are you worried?"

"Of course, I am. I'm in my fifties and live alone. I have a few valuable things lying around. It would be stupid not to worry."

Something I wasn't concerned about. With little of value in my apartment and a dog the size of a small donkey, I slept well at night. I switched direction and drove to the local animal shelter where barks greeted us as we exited the car. "Stay, Sheba." No sense in the dogs not chosen feeling bad. "We won't be long."

The three of us entered the office section where a young woman barely glanced up and waved us to the door marked dogs. Through there were three signs—small, medium, and large pointing to different doors.

"An ankle biter would be as much of a warning as a big dog, right?" Shar headed for the farthest door.

"Yes, but it can't provide a lot of protection," Mom said. "Honey is considered a medium dog, but her teeth are sharp. She could do serious damage to someone's calf."

More often than not, the conversation between my friend and my mother was the most entertaining part of my day. I suppressed a grin and let them lead the way.

"All I need is a warning, not a killer." Shar peered into each cage. "Something cute that doesn't shed."

"A poodle, schnauzer, or mix of the two?" I suggested.

She stopped in front of a cage containing a silver poodle. Bug-eyed with a big tongue protruding from her mouth, the dog yipped and wagged her tail.

"This one."

Mom narrowed her eyes. "She's, uh, kind of ugly."

"Beauty is in the eye of the beholder," Shar said. "Not being the prettiest will make her more loyal. I've learned that from experience."

I exchanged an amused glance with Mom. I didn't understand Shar's reasoning, but most people did tend to gravitate to the cuter dogs. "She'll be very happy with you. I'll let the girl up front know." At the front desk, I cleared my throat several times before she glanced up. "We've made our choice."

"Okay. I'll be there in a minute." She glanced at her cell phone.

"Have you had a rash of dogs brought in today?"

"A few that were picked up from a farm outside of town, why?"

"From a dog-fighting ring?"

She shrugged. "They bear some scars. If you're that interested, check out the cages through the big dog door."

Since she didn't seem in a big hurry to help Shar, I decided to do just that. Loud barks greeted me as I opened the door. At the far end were four cages. On those cages hung signs that read these animals weren't yet available for adoption. A pit bull, two mixed breeds, and a rottweiler, all bearing battle scars.

My heart sank, knowing the other dogs had been put down. "Good luck, y'all. I hope you are able to find good homes and forget the trauma of your past." I stretched a hand toward one of the cages only to have the dog growl and lunge. "Yep, you're going to need all the luck you can get." I prayed for a miracle.

By the time I rejoined the others, Shar held the poodle in her arms. "The sign said her name is Starr. I like it."

"Let's see how she acts with the other animals."

After Shar paid, we headed back to the car where Shar climbed in the backseat. Starr immediately started yelping and climbing all over my patient mastiff. Poor Sheba huffed and laid her head on her paws.

"They're going to be best friends," Shar said.

I doubted that, but my dog would tolerate hers.

"I'll have just enough time to bathe and groom her before my first appointment. Purple ribbons and nail polish will go well with her silver coat."

Mercy. A frou-frou dog.

At the store, Heather raised her eyebrows as Shar carried Starr to the back. "I never expected that."

"She's worried about the thefts."

"And she thinks a tiny poodle will keep her safe?"

I shrugged. "You know Shar."

"Now what?" Mom asked. "We visited the latest victim, so what's our next step?"

"We keep an eye out for a large man with the unique shoe tread I showed you."

"So, we're supposed to go around and ask men to show us the bottom of their shoe?"

"Of course, not. We pay attention to footprints in the dirt." I chuckled. "We'll find him or he'll find us." I hoped for the first, which was only marginally better than the second option. Either way, when we found the culprit, they wouldn't be happy.

After locking up the store at five o'clock, I declined supper with my parents, wanting nothing more than to curl up with my fur babies and watch TV. After too many late nights, I needed to go to bed early.

Brad called right before my show ended. I paused the movie. "Hey."

"Ready for me to come home?"

"I was ready five minutes after you left." I

stretched out, propping a throw pillow behind my head.

"I'll be there early enough to bring you coffee."

"Sounds perfect."

I fell asleep soon after the call, waking to my phone ringing and the movie still paused. "Hello?"

"I need you to come over right now."

"Shar?" I sat up. "Why are you whispering?"

"Someone is in my house. Alex isn't answering his phone. Starr is hiding under the covers. Bring Sheba." Click.

I bolted off the sofa, slid my feet into my gym shoes, grabbed my gun, and then raced out the door calling for Sheba to follow. While I headed for my car, I sent a text to McIlroy asking him to meet me there. I broke every speed limit between my house and Shar's, parking in front of the house next door. Grabbing a flashlight from the glove compartment, I snuck down the sidewalk toward Shar's plantation-style home. No lights shone in the house.

"Come on, girl. We have a friend to save." I darted toward the house, staying as much to the shadows as possible. Where was McIlroy?

I crept around the outside of the house, looking for an open door or window. The moonless night made it impossible to make out footprints in any of the flower beds, and the lack of rain had the ground too hard anyway.

I froze when a twig snapped under my feet. Not hearing the sound of pounding feet running from the house, I continued to the kitchen door. Locked. Thankfully, Shar and I had keys to each other's houses. I dug mine from my pocket and slipped inside, letting Sheba go first.

The very thing my friend had feared had happened. She'd been targeted.

A thud sounded from the living room. I motioned for Sheba to check it out. When I entered the room, I clicked on my flashlight. Nothing but fluttering curtains at the open window and a book on the floor.

I stared at the scantily dressed couple on the cover. Shar's taste in reading leaned on the steamy side. "Shar?"

"Don't call out. Someone is in the office."

Sheba took off like a shot.

A man cried out.

Glass shattered.

I rushed into the room in time to see a slim leg disappear out the broken window. "Stop." Too late, I peered outside to see a young man in jeans and a dark hoodie race into the trees. The red and blue flashing lights of an arriving squad car broke through the darkness. About time.

"You can come out now," I said. "He got away."

"My dog is worthless." Shar carried a trembling Starr down the stairs. "At the first thud, she yelped and hid."

"You have three days to return her." I stuck my gun in the waistband of my pants.

"Never. I love her." She glared at the broken window. "Guess I need to see whether anything is missing."

"Shar?" McIlroy rushed into the room. "Are you okay?"

"I tried to call you."

"Sorry. I was so tired I fell asleep with my phone in another room. I checked it when I got up to use the restroom." He pulled her close.

"Yes, I'm fine. Trinity chased the thief away."

Starr growled and snapped at McIlroy.

"Whoa. What's this?"

"A dog who doesn't know friend from foe." Shar kissed the top of the dog's fuzzy head and set her on the floor. "Be nice."

"Tell me what happened." Alex led her to the sofa.

"I was sleeping, but a noise woke me up. I sat up and heard the sound of someone sneaking around. Tried to call you, then called Trinity, who came right over." She narrowed her eyes.

"I said I was sorry. All these buglaries have worn me out." He took her hand in his. "Thank you, Trinity."

"Well, I didn't do much but chase him off, or rather Sheba did."

"Nothing appears to be missing," Shar said.

"I didn't see him carrying anything. It was definitely a guy wearing jeans and a dark hoodie. I checked the perimeter before entering the house but didn't see any tracks. He fled into the woods. I didn't see his face or anything to identify him."

The detective shook his head. "The crime is increasing. Barely a night goes by without a call like this. We need help. I'll be hunting for another officer first thing tomorrow. For now, Shar is staying with me. She might not be so lucky next time."

"Can't I stay with Trinity?"

Surprise crossed his face. "You'd rather stay with her than me?"

"Only because you'll try to keep me from investigating further."

He bolted to his feet. "You beat all I've ever seen. Of course, I will. In case you've forgotten already, someone broke into your house while you lay sleeping upstairs." His face darkened. "The safest place for you is in the house of law enforcement. Or jail. Take your pick."

She stood and faced him, their noses almost touching. "On what grounds?"

"Impeding an investigation and the potential to harm yourself."

Oh, boy. This was not going well. I glanced from one to the other wanting to diffuse the situation and having no idea how. "Uh, can I go now?"

When neither of them looked my way, I slipped out the front door McIlroy had left open in his haste. As I started closing it behind me, I heard him agree to stay with her in her place. Smiling, I headed home.

Chapter Nine

"Good morning."

I wasn't greeted by coffee but a kiss gently placed on my lips as I slept. "Brad." I wrapped my arms around his neck. "What a way to wake up." I bolted to a sitting position, my forehead colliding with his. "Ow. Am I late? Did I oversleep?"

"No." He rubbed his head. "Thought I'd surprise you and spend a few minutes here before heading to work. I'll still bring the coffee."

I gave a sheepish grin. "Sorry about the head butt. Want to try again?"

Smiling, he leaned over and kissed me again. "You were out. What did you do last night?"

Tossing aside the sheet, I smiled as his gaze roamed over my legs revealed by the shorts I wore to bed. "Shar's house was broken into. When she couldn't get a hold of McIlroy, she called me. I took Sheba over, and we chased away the bad guy. McIlroy is staying with her for a while."

"That's sound like a good idea. You should move into my guestroom again."

"No thanks, I'm safe here. I'm not an elderly woman, and I have a big dog. Not to mention two ferocious cats."

"Your cats would run and hide at the first sign of trouble. Thank you for taking care of Barney." He reached down and petted the pup he'd let out of his crate. "He's already been out, and the animals have been fed. Feel up to an omelet? I'll cook."

"I can't resist your omelets, and Barney is progressing nicely with his collar. I haven't had to shock him once, but I do use the vibrate button a lot." Taking Brad's hand, I led him to the kitchen. I took a seat at the breakfast bar and watched him gather the preparations for breakfast.

"With you taking down the dog ring and now the burglaries," he said, pulling a pan from the cupboard, "I'm not comfortable leaving you here."

"The two aren't related."

"How do you know? It probably takes a lot of money to run that ring. They could be funding it by stealing." He cracked eggs into a bowl. "Someone out there could be mad at you for ending their lifestyle."

"I do have a tendency to get on the wrong side of bad guys."

He glanced over his shoulder. "I'm not joking."

No, he wasn't. I recognized the hard, yet worried look in his eyes. "I'm sorry. I'm not focusing on anything but the burglaries now. With someone breaking into Shar's home, it's personal."

"I understand that, but..." he returned to

cooking not needing to finish his sentence.

I knew what he meant. Soon I'd be neck deep in troubled water again, if I wasn't already.

The delicious aroma of frying bacon filled the kitchen. There was nothing sexier than a man waking a woman with a kiss and then cooking her breakfast.

Barney leaned on Brad's leg, while Sheba stared up at him with big eyes, both begging for a bite of bacon. Brad smiled and obliged, breaking the first cooked piece in half. "That's all you get. Now out of the kitchen."

Sheba obeyed, but Barney barked.

"The remote is here." I handed it to Brad. "He might as well get used to you training him."

"Out." Brad pointed. The pup looked at the remote in his hand and scampered away. "Look at that. I didn't have to push the button."

"He's a smart little guy, if not a bit stubborn." I eyed the fringe of an afghan that had hung too close to his cage. Barney had pulled as much of it through as he could and made himself a bed.

"I think I'll take him to work with me today and see how he does." Brad handed me a plate with a bacon and cheese omelet. "It'd be nice to have him trained well enough to keep me company in the office."

"Moses could do that."

"Nah." Brad shook his head. "Ever since my kidnapping when the theater was under construction, Moses hates the place. Barney hasn't experienced trouble there, so hopefully he'll settle right in."

"Make sure you have plenty of chew toys." Otherwise, Brad would be replacing some of his expensive leather furniture.

After we ate and I'd showered, Brad went to buy coffee, leaving me to unlock the store. A cardboard box sat on the sidewalk. Experience had taught me to be very careful.

I unlocked the front door and stared at the box, tempted to call McIlroy instead of opening it. The meowing of kittens made my decision. I hated when people dumped animals on my doorstep.

I unfolded the tabs holding the box closed and stared at a trio of tuxedo kittens. A sheet of white copy paper glared from the bottom of the box. With a trembling hand, I pulled the paper out and read, "Since you're such an animal lover, consider these cats lucky. Back away or next time they go in a burlap sack into the lake."

Glancing around to see if whoever had left the note still lurked around, I carried everything inside. The kittens went into a cage with a For Sale sign. The paper I set on the counter before calling McIlroy.

I left a voice mail and glanced across the parking lot to see Brad heading my way, his hands full of coffee cups. The note would only enforce his wanting me to stay with him. I had before, so doing so again shouldn't be such a big deal, but I really loved my independence. What if he asked me to marry him someday? I knew I'd say yes but couldn't shove aside the notion that I might not be in control of my own life.

A stupid thought, really. Dad didn't dictate

Mom's actions. He wouldn't dare. I pasted on a smile, knowing I had some deep soul searching to do. I'd been single for so long, I still wasn't used to the fact that a desirable man loved me.

"What's wrong?" Brad asked after immediately entering the store.

Why did my emotions show so plainly on my face? I motioned to the paper and accepted the coffee meant for me, setting the others aside for Heather and Shar.

Brad read the note and sighed. "At least the threat wasn't toward you."

"No, just helpless animals. You're right. The dog ring and the robberies must be connected." I shuddered. With Jones behind bars, who ran the show now?

McIlroy arrived with Shar, Heather a few seconds behind them. "Where's the note?" The detective went straight to business.

I handed it to him while Brad explained his thoughts. "Maybe you can talk some sense into Trinity so she'll move to the penthouse until this is over."

McIlroy nodded. "The threat might not be directly aimed at you, but you have pets. Why risk them?"

The thought of my fur babies being in danger made the decision for me. "I'll move in until this is over."

"It's not a big deal," Shar said. "Alex is with me, although I got up early to make sure I had makeup on before he woke up."

McIlroy shook his head. "As if it matters to me.

The worst part of staying over is the hard mattress on your guest bed. Like I've said before, ladies, no one goes anywhere alone." He gave Shar a quick kiss and strolled from the store.

"Do you think I'm in danger?" Heather paled. "I don't fit the victimology, but—"

"I don't think so," I said. "No offense, but they're targeting older women with money."

"True. That doesn't fit me. I live paycheck to paycheck." Her eyes widened. "I didn't mean you don't pay me well. It's just that with my ex in prison, there's no child support for another two years."

"Watch out for each other." Brad kissed me, petted Sheba, and took Barney across the parking lot with him.

"The store will be a lot quieter without that beagle," Shar said. "I have a full schedule today, so I'm heading to the grooming room. If Lou shows up, tell her I can't go sleuthing. Besides, I was the one broken into last night. No need to rehash the event."

Mom wasn't pleased when she arrived, and I told her. She glared toward the grooming room. "But I have a lead. Well, more like an idea. Your father is going to the gym on a regular basis to look for a shoe with the tread pattern you found."

"That's a good idea. Tell Dad to observe, not confront."

"He's not an idiot, dear." She plopped in a chair by the window. "I'll think on what our next move should be."

I left her to her devices, made sure the ad for

kittens and chihuahua puppies still ran online, and paid some bills. We only had two puppies left, and I expected them to be gone soon. Whenever I glanced up from my work, Mom either doodled on the paper in front of her or stared out the window.

"How long is Dad going to stay at the gym?"

"As long as it takes."

I widened my eyes. "He actually thinks he'll find the man we're looking for?"

"Where else do men hang out around here?"

"Bars." Waterfall had two, but our guy might not be from our town.

"Fishing tournaments," Heather said. "Cornhole competitions."

Mom's shoulders sagged. "It'll take a month of Sundays to search all those places. We'll hit one of the bars tonight but no skimpy dresses, Trinity. I've never been so embarrassed. Why can't Brad invite us to the country club? Maybe we'll get lucky and can dress up at the same time?"

"I didn't see anyone at that barn who looked like country club material."

"Then, we'll simply enjoy a nice dinner. Why else date a rich man, dear, if not to enjoy the finer things in life?"

I opened and closed my mouth a few times, not believing what I heard. "I'm not dating Brad because of his money."

"Oh, I know that." She waved a dismissive hand. "But, why not enjoy the benefits?"

"I enjoy them plenty." I pounded away at my keyboard, deleting more invoices than I saved. Giving up, I said, "Fine, I'll mention dinner to him."

"Buy yourself a new dress."

"The dresses I have are fine." Although I hadn't visited the thrift store in a while. Someone Else's Junk did carry some nice things. "Why don't you go see whether Mrs. Murdoch recognizes the shoe pattern?" Anything to give me a few minutes' respite.

"That idea is better than sitting around here twiddling my thumbs." Mom marched from the store.

Mom returned half an hour later, excitement vibrating from every line of her body. "Bingo. Mrs. Murdoch said she sold a pair of shoes that matched that tread two weeks ago. She'd gotten a shipment of new, overstocked sneakers in."

"Who did she sell them to?" I rose to my feet and reached for my phone.

"A big guy. Said she remembered him because of his size and unfriendliness. He bought the shoes and a trench coat."

"A trench coat?" I frowned. "Did she have a name?"

"She has to go through her receipts and will call you if she finds his." Looking pleased with herself, Mom sat back in the chair she'd vacated earlier. "I make a pretty good detective, don't I? Haven't had this much fun in ages."

"Mom, you're the best." I grinned.

My cell phone rang. "Tail Waggin'. How may I help you?"

"This is Mrs. Murdoch. The name of the man who bought the size twelve shoes is Donald Wright.

He owns some chicken houses about ten miles out of town."

Chapter Ten

I hung up and told Mom her bit of scouting had worked. "A good day's work."

"What are you saying?" She grabbed her purse. "We need to visit those chicken houses."

"Nope. I'll pass this info on to McIlroy." I sent her a hard look that I hoped showed I meant business. "Isn't dinner at the country club enough of a plan for later in the day?"

"That's later. I'm talking about now. Think I'm in the market for some fresh eggs." She slung her purse over her shoulder.

"Stop. You don't waltz up to a chicken house to buy eggs. They're usually shipped somewhere else."

"But, I don't know that, do I?" She tilted her head and grinned. "I'm new to the area and not familiar with how things work."

"I grew up here." I wanted to bang my head against the countertop.

"That Wright man won't know that."

Someone needed to talk reason to her, and she wasn't listening to me. "I'm calling Dad." I grabbed my cell phone.

"He's next door on a mission. Stop being a ninny. I'll be fine." She marched out the front door.

I jumped up, rushing past a wide-eyed Heather, and gave chase, dialing Dad as I went. Then I planted myself in front of Mom's car. "Dad, Mom has lost her mind. You need to come out here."

"What's she done now?"

"She wants to go snooping alone at the farm of a strong suspect. I'm blocking her car." I put a hand on the hood. Since my car was behind hers, she couldn't go anywhere unless she ran me over.

"I see her." Dad waved from the gym window. "Be right there."

"Lou, sweetie, is this some kind of mid-life crises?" Dad leaned in her open window. "Let me buy you an ice cream."

"I'm not a child, Joe. You told me to find a hobby. This is it." She frowned.

"Couldn't you have taken up knitting?"

Uh-oh. One of the worst things Dad could do was talk to Mom as if she was a child or a female.

Her face darkened. "Move out of the way, Trinity."

"I'm calling the detective." I dialed McIlroy. "Mom has lost her mind." I quickly explained the situation.

"I'm pulling into the parking lot now." His car pulled alongside Mom's. Crisis averted.

"Get out of the car, Mrs. Ashford." McIlroy

motioned to her. "I'll handle the chicken farmer. You did great giving me that information."

Mom started to look a little more appeased but still sat rigid in the driver's seat.

"I have something I'd like you to do for me."

She cut the detective a sideways glance. "I'm listening."

"My receptionist is out for a while due to a family issue. Would you be willing to fill in for her? A woman with your smarts could fill her shoes easily."

I didn't think it a good idea. Mom would be privy to all sorts of information that could send her straight on a path to danger. She'd think it the duty of the Waterfall Sleuths to help with any case that came into the station.

Mom brightened and exited the car. "Finally, someone sees my worth. I'll start in the morning." She tossed me a haughty look, breezed past Dad, and flounced back into the store.

"Thank you." Dad thrust out his hand. "She's been searching for a purpose since we settled down. Thinks she's found it by being a solver of mysteries, Lord help us."

McIlroy shook his hand. "No problem. I am in need of someone to man the front desk. Hopefully, that will keep her out of trouble."

"It'll thrust her into more," I said. "She'll be answering the phones."

"Most of my cases come through email. She won't see them." He grinned and went in search of Shar.

I made a move to follow, then spotted Brad

dashing around the corner of the theater. A few seconds later, Barney crawled from underneath a parked car. The little troublemaker. "Catch up to you later, Dad."

I jogged toward the beagle, keeping an eye out for moving vehicles. It wouldn't be good if either one of us were run over. "Here, Barney."

The dog raced away toward the alley behind the buildings. I increased my speed feeling the effects of my lackadaisical attitude toward the gym almost immediately. Time to get back on the treadmill on a regular basis. This intermittent visiting wouldn't do at all. "Barney!" I turned the corner and rammed into Brad.

"Oof." His arms wrapped around me, keeping us both from falling.

"Where's the remote to his collar?"

"He isn't paying any attention to it. The little rascal took off, nose to the ground about fifteen minutes ago." Brad released me. "He's definitely onto something."

"A hotdog in the trash, probably." I smiled. "Let's find your dog."

We'd catch glimpses of him as he ran, nose down the length of the alley. Suddenly, he stopped and barked as a black truck sped from the alley.

"He doesn't seem to like the driver of that truck." I glanced at Brad. "Do you think it could be the man he stole the watch from?" We really needed to find out who dropped Barney off on my doorstep. I mentioned the idea to Brad.

"Maybe." He quirked his mouth. "Let me ask around to see who might have once owned this beagle."

"Who could you possibly ask?"

He shrugged. "Maybe an ad in the local paper. A call to a few breeders. I'll let you know what I find." He called again to Barney who followed orders this time. Brad clipped a leash to his collar. "Come on, boy, before you actually get into trouble."

"Oh, Mom wants you to take us all to the club for supper tonight. Are you free?"

"Sounds good." He leaned down and kissed me. "See you at six."

I returned to the store and let Mom know she could dress nice that evening.

"Oh, good. I'm going to get my hair styled, buy some work clothes—that sort of thing. See you later." She bustled away on errands that wouldn't get her into trouble.

I returned to work with peace of mind, selling the last of the chihuahua puppies and kittens, then wrote a check to the local shelter.

A few minutes before closing time, Brad arrived. "Want to visit a beagle breeder with me? One of them I called said she might recognize Barney and could tell me who purchased him."

"Sure. I can close early. Heather?"

"I have a date with David, so leaving early is fine by me." She grinned and grabbed her purse. "Shar is already gone. Said McIlroy is grilling steaks for her."

An all-around date night for everyone it seemed. "I'll need to be back in time to get ready."

"We will be." Brad took my hand and led me to

the car, Sheba padding along behind us.

I put her in the backseat with the squirming beagle, then climbed into the front passenger seat. "I see you put a pet cover over your leather seats."

"Since my dog can't be still, I was afraid his nails would damage them."

"Smart thinking. How much has he chewed up at home?"

"An expensive pair of Italian shoes and the corner of my favorite chair. I'm hoping he'll outgrow that type of behavior."

"You can't let him run free until he's trained."

"Has he ever given you that poor-me look?" Brad shook his head. "I can't resist those eyes. Kind of like when you look at me wanting something."

I playfully slapped his shoulder. "I do not have beagle eyes."

"You might as well. I can't resist you either." Laughing, he drove to the interstate and headed south.

The breeder's small country house sat about half a mile from the road across the railroad tracks. A sprawling outbuilding sat off to one side, a pasture with cows and a pond on the other. The type of property I envisioned myself owning someday but with a larger house. I did want children in the future.

A couple in their sixties, Mr. and Mrs. McGee, sat in rocking chairs on the front porch and stood as we approached. The man smiled, seeing Barney scampering beside Brad. "Oh, yes, I remember this little fella. He's the spitting image of his father. Want to see?"

We nodded and followed him to the outbuilding where rows of pens containing beagles were. "Our dogs are registered with good bloodlines. This pup here came from this handsome boy."

I gazed on the spitting image of Barney. "Was he a handful as a puppy, too? Barney likes to run and take things that aren't his."

"Oh, yes. Big Daddy—that's his name because of how large his feet were as a puppy—got into all kinds of trouble."

"Do you remember who you sold my dog to?"

"I keep impeccable records. Mind telling me how you got a hold of him?"

"Someone dropped him off at my pet store," I said.

His eyes flashed. "After paying six-hundred-dollars for him, you'd think they'd have more sense. Come to the house. I'll look up the name of the purchaser."

I gripped Brad's hand. "You won't give him up, will you?"

"No. They lost their chance with him when they dumped him." He gave my hand a squeeze.

Mr. McGee led us to a small home office where his wife greeted us with sweet tea and cookies. "Here you go. The man who bought him was John Flamell."

I gave Brad a startled look. "Flamell?"

Mr. McGee nodded. "Said the dog was a gift for his wife."

Because she'd given him a Rolex? "Thank you. I know Mrs. Flamell. You've been very helpful."

"I'll not sell her another. Feel free to tell her

that." He slammed the folder closed. "You've a good dog there once he's older. If you ever want to breed that mastiff, let me know. I know a guy with a gorgeous male."

We thanked him and hurried back to the car. "Do we have time to squeeze in a visit to Margie?" I asked.

"We'll make time."

Twenty minutes later, we pulled in front of Margie's house. I sent a text to Mom and Dad saying it would be closer to six-thirty when we picked them up. I was serious about needing time to get ready. I couldn't very well wear jeans and a tee-shirt.

Margie greeted us at the door. "Did you find my watch?"

I narrowed my eyes. "No, but we did discover that this dog—" I pointed to Barney, "belonged to your husband. Mind telling me why he was dumped at my store?"

She sighed. "My husband is dead. This dog reminded me of that every time I looked at him. I don't have time to train a puppy, Miss Ashford."

I'd think that being a widow would be enough of a reminder that her husband had died. "But why dump him?"

"Easier and faster." She shrugged. "I wasn't thinking clearly in my grief."

"Are you aware that this dog is the one who found your husband's missing watch at the lake?"

Surprise flickered across her face. "This little thing is the one who found it? Any idea when the police will release the watch back to me?"

"No," Brad said. "Ma'am, I think it's against the law to dump animals, even in front of a pet store. I hope you aren't intending to take him back because I won't release him to you. The dog is mine now."

"I don't suppose you'd pay me for him?" She smiled.

"Not a chance." He whirled and marched back to the car.

I studied Mrs. Flamell. She didn't seem the grieving-widow type to me. I'd seen the greedy look in her eyes when she'd asked about the watch and Brad giving her money for Barney.

Something dirty roamed these hills, and I intended to find out what.

Chapter Eleven

"She's lying." I sipped my crystal goblet of water, peering over the rim at the others.

"Who, dear?" Mom frowned.

"Margie Flamell. She seems more concerned with money than her husband's death. Do we know how he died?"

They all looked at each other before Brad spoke. "I don't think so. She only mentioned that he was dead."

Excusing myself, I hurried to the women's restroom to call McIlroy. I found few things less annoying than someone on their phone in a restaurant.

"Please don't tell me you found a dead body."

"No, actually, I'm looking for one." I smiled. "How did John Flamell die?"

"The husband of the woman who'd been burglarized? Hold on."

I could hear the rustling of papers and the typing

of a keyboard before McIlroy talked to me. "It only shows him as missing, presumed dead. We haven't really looked into it because Mrs. Flamell doesn't seem very concerned. I figured he took off for a while."

"Then why try to act like a grieving widow and get rid of his things?"

"Maybe they had a huge fight. Unless we find evidence of foul play, we can't do anything."

I thanked him and hung up, leaning against the bathroom counter. What kind of game was Margie playing?

I jerked as a woman came out of one of the stalls. I recognized her type. Young, pretty, the perfect arm candy for a wealthy man, plus I actually knew her as the girlfriend of the man who owned the gym next to Tail Waggin'. "Hello, Amber. How's Joe Evans?"

"Fine." She waved her left hand. A huge diamond flashed from her finger.

"Congratulations." She'd done it. Found a wealthy man to make an honest woman out of her.

"Thank you." She turned on the faucet. "I couldn't help but overhear your phone conversation, and as you know, I'm acquainted with a lot of people around here, the Flamells included."

"Really?" I met her gaze in the mirror. "Well?"

"This is only gossip, mind you. I have no proof, but I've heard the Flamells, once one of the area's wealthiest families, has fallen on hard times."

"Please don't tell me gambling." I've dealt with people with that affliction too many times, including Heather's ex-husband.

"No one seems to know other than the husband applied for several loans and was denied on every one of them." She grabbed a paper towel and dried her hands. "They used to own hundreds of acres of prime timberland up on the mountain but used it as collateral a few years back and lost it."

"How do you know all this?"

"Pillow talk, darling." She patted my cheek. Actually patted my cheek.

I glared. "Why would Evans care?"

"Because he now owns that prime timber land." Her scarlet grin widened. "He's thinking of building a golf resort."

"Heaven forbid." Why did people want to spoil the beauty of small-town living with big city monstrosities? Sure, it provided jobs, but to gouge a space out of a mountain... "Thanks for the info. Please call me if you think of anything else."

"Don't you want to know my thoughts on Mr. Flamell's whereabouts?"

"Do you know something?"

"Let's just say he was at Leroy's Bar one night and went missing the next morning." She tossed me a wiggle of her fingers and sashayed out the door.

I hurried back to the table and recounted what I'd learned. "Looks like we're headed to Leroy's tomorrow night."

"Why not now? The night is young," Mom said. "We can eat and skedaddle. I doubt we'll learn anything more here. Isn't it amazing how informative these girlfriends can be? I remember the day when I could convince a man to tell me anything."

"You still have that effect on me." Dad leaned over and kissed her cheek.

Mom blushed. "Oh, go on."

"I guess we could head to Leroy's," Brad said. "We're a bit overdressed, though."

I glanced at the simple black sheath I wore. "Would we have time to change? It's a country and western place, right?"

He nodded and motioned for the bill. "It's a popular place. We'll be lucky to get a table this late in the evening."

"We'll belly up to the bar if we have to," Dad said, helping Mom to her feet.

An hour later, dressed in jeans and a gauzy blouse with a tank underneath, I entered the bar on Brad's arm. He wore jeans and a button-up shirt. I wasn't sure if he was sexier in jeans or a suit. All I knew was that every woman in the place eyed him with hungry eyes. Head high I let him lead me to a table in the corner.

Sawdust covered the scarred wooden floors. A band played popular country tunes while multiple couples two-stepped around the dance floor.

"Look how the ladies stare at you, Joe." Mom hugged his arm.

Dad laughed. "They're looking at Brad, but thank you, sweetheart."

Brad leaned over and whispered in my ear, "I want to be like your parents when we're old."

My face flushed. His statement told me for certain he planned on us having a future. I curled my fingers around my engagement ring. Amber and Evans had nothing in comparison. Maybe the love she had for him matched what I had for Brad, but I couldn't imagine anything as strong.

"What do we do now?" Mom asked. "We can't stand up and ask who knows what happened to John Flamell."

"Of course not." I shrugged. "First, we look and listen. Subtly ask questions of the waitress. Let Brad handle that part. Women respond well to him, where I come across as nosy."

"You do have an abrasive side," Mom said.

I opened my mouth to protest, then decided it wasn't worth the trouble. Nosy and abrasive were not the same thing.

"What can I get you folks?" A waitress in her late twenties, hair teased so high it looked like yellow cotton candy, stood next to our table. While her question included us all, her gaze settled on Brad.

He smiled and ordered drinks. I chose a soda, wanting to keep my wits about me. Since I was once again involved in a mystery, bad things tended to happen when I let my guard down.

Content to let Brad handle things, I relaxed and watched the dancers. I didn't recognize anyone and couldn't help but wonder whether we were wasting our time. Not that the night was late at only eight o'clock, but my bed was calling to me right now.

"Let's dance before you fall asleep." Brad pulled me to my feet and onto the dance floor as the band played a slow song.

I let the music and the feel of his arms sweep me away. Yes, we were there to find out about Margie's husband, but things were far better swaying with Brad.

Shouts alerted us to a fight breaking out across the room. Brad stepped in front of me, placing himself between me and possible danger.

I peered around him to see the very man we'd been looking for—chicken farmer, Donald Wright—throw a punch at a much younger man. I couldn't tell who had the upper hand, the larger farmer or the younger man who had a shrieking woman cowering behind a table.

Two bouncers rushed forward and broke up the fight. Wright tried punching around them until a bouncer wrapped a strong arm around the man's neck and dragged him toward the door.

"This place is more exciting than the country club," Mom said, joining us on the dance floor.

"I doubt those stuffed shirts at the club would dare cause a ruckus." Dad put an arm around her shoulders. "They wouldn't or the club would ban them."

"Should we follow Wright?" I glanced up at Brad. "He is the man we're looking for."

"Him and Flamell." Brad took my hand and wove in and out of those returning to the dance floor. We reached the door and fresh air.

Wright, cursing and waving his arms around, stumbled toward a big black truck. He caught us watching, said something I couldn't decipher, and climbed into the driver's seat.

"That man should not be driving," Mom said. "Call that detective. Maybe they can head him off."

"Rickson will." I motioned to where a squad car sat parked at the edge of the lot. "They must survey the area frequently to prevent drunk driving."

Rickson moved his car forward, blocking Wright from exiting, then exited his car. "Step out, sir. I cannot let you drive out of here. We'll call you a cab."

"Ain't no cabs around here." Wright gunned the engine. "Move or I'll run you down."

Rickson put his hand on the gun at his hip. "Please step out of the car."

My heart lodged in my throat. This would not go well. "What can we do?"

"Nothing." Brad held tight to my hand. "Except call McIlroy and let him know what's happening."

"I'm filming this." Mom pulled her cell phone from the small clutch she carried. "We might need the evidence. Young people do this all the time. I've seen it online."

A good idea, actually. I kept my attention on Rickson.

A gunshot pierced the air.

Rickson fell.

Wright's truck rammed the squad car, then turned and squealed tires out of the parking lot.

We sprinted toward Rickson.

Brad fell to his knees beside the fallen officer. "Joe, call the police. Trinity, hand me your blouse. He's alive but losing a lot of blood. The shot took him in the shoulder."

Grateful for the tank top I'd worn under the sheer blouse, I peeled off the outer layer and handed it to Brad. He pressed it against the wound as Dad called the police.

By now, a crowd had gathered, including the

waitress who had served us our drinks. "Does this happen a lot?" I asked. "Fights and gunfire?"

"Only when Wright shows up. The last time we had a fight here was the night a man named Flamell disappeared."

"He fought with Wright?"

"Yeah, over some floozy who only comes here to pick up men so drunk they don't know what they're doing."

"Do you know the woman's name?"

She narrowed her eyes. "Why so many questions?"

"We're trying to find out what happened to Flamell."

"Her name is Carol Turner. Lives in the trailer park on the east end of Waterfall. An aging beauty pageant winner who can't let go of a lifestyle that no longer suits her. She was hanging all over Flamell that night and Wright, who thinks she is his girl, took offense. Be careful of that man. He's a mean one." She turned and returned to the bar.

Less than ten minutes later, McIlroy, followed by an ambulance, roared into the lot. The detective glanced my way and shook his head, no doubt thinking trouble followed wherever I went. He wouldn't be too far off the mark. It did seem that way to me more often than not.

Brad wiped his hands on a towel handed to him by one of the paramedics and stepped back to let them do their job.

"You most likely saved this officer's life," one of them said. "Good job."

McIlroy followed Brad to us. "Tell me what

happened. Brad only. I don't need all of you talking at once."

"Wright got into a fight with another man inside. A bouncer dragged Wright outside—he was very drunk. Rickson tried to stop him from driving and was shot. That sums it up."

"Other man still inside?"

"That's him leaning against that blue sedan." Brad motioned his head to where the other man and the woman he was with watched the proceedings. "I don't know what prompted the fight."

"Last time Wright was in a fight," I said, "it was over a woman. That fight was with John Flamell. Wright might be the last person who saw him alive. We need to visit this Carol woman."

Chapter Twelve

According to McIlroy, Rickson would survive. The bullet had gone straight through. Bad news was it left our small, local police department even more short-handed. Which convinced my mother we were needed now more than ever if Wright was to be brought to justice.

"I had this same conversation with your father last night," she said, sipping her coffee at the table next to my store's front window. "And I spoke to Shar early this morning. This town needs the Waterfall Sleuths to step up their game."

"I agree." Shar nodded. "Leave the store to Heather and let's visit Carol Turner. We're going whether you choose to join us or not."

Knowing someone with a level head needed to accompany them, I agreed. "As long as Sheba goes with us. I'm not going to confront a potential killer without her protection."

"I'm packin'," Mom said.

"Me, too," Shar added.

"I have mine, but Sheba is an early warning signal." McIlroy would have a brain aneurysm if he knew the three of us were toting guns and questioning the girlfriend of a potential murderer. Maybe he'd grown used to our shenanigans. I glanced at Heather.

"Go on. I can man the store without y'all." Her lips thinned.

"We can go later. I hate being away from work so much." I tried to meet her gaze. When she ducked her head, I asked, "Are you all right?"

Tears welled in her eyes. "David asked me to marry him last night."

"That's great." I rushed to wrap her in a hug. "Isn't it?"

She sniffed and shrugged. "After Bobby, I'm worried that I might be a bad judge of character in men. Plus, it's kind of soon, isn't it?"

"You're a great judge of character." I held her at arm's length and stared into her eyes. "David is a great man. You've known him for a long time. So what if you've only dated a few months. Have a long engagement if it makes you feel better, but do not let him get away. Think of how pretty your babies will be. His dark skin and curly hair, your pale skin and hint of auburn. Gorgeous."

She laughed and wiped her eyes on her sleeve. "It's way too early to think of babies."

When David arrived a few minutes later with the day's delivery of supplies, we all turned and grinned. He paused in the doorway. "What?"

"Nothing," we said in unison.

CYNTHIA HICKEY

I patted Heather on the shoulder. "Remember what I said," I whispered, then motioned my head for Mom and Shar to follow me, snapped my fingers for Sheba, and left the two lovebirds alone. A grin spread across my face. After all the trouble Heather's first husband had put her through, she needed a good man like David.

I sent a text to Brad, letting him know where we were going, then let Sheba into the backseat of my car with Mom who didn't mind a little dog hair on her clothes. Brad replied to be careful and make sure the tracker on my phone was on.

I checked, it was, and turned toward the trailer park on the east side of town, my mind working on a way to broach the subject of Carol flirting with a married man while dating a volatile one. Chances were strong she'd refuse to answer our questions. If she did, we'd need something to hold over her in order to persuade her to talk.

"You're awful quiet up there," Mom said.

"Just thinking of a way to coerce Carol to talk if she refuses."

"That's easy. Threaten her with Margie. I bet she doesn't think the wife knows about her and the philandering John. Maybe Margie does, maybe she doesn't."

"Good head, Lou." Shar nodded. "We'll make her talk. You can always sic Sheba on her."

My mouth gaped. "On an innocent woman?"

"Innocent, my patooty."

"Well, she isn't Donald Wright, and he's the one we're after." I turned into the Waterfall Trailer Park. "Anyone know which one is hers?"

They both shook their heads. I sighed and parked in front of the manager's office. "I'll be right back."

The bored woman behind the desk didn't look up when she told me Carol lived in number fifteen. "You'll probably wake her up. She works nights."

"Thanks." I returned to my car and drove to the correct trailer.

Carol wasn't sleeping. She sat outside in a robe and nightgown that barely covered what should be hidden and smoked a cigarette. Dyed platinum blond hair scrunched into a messy bun. Smeared mascara lined blue eyes, and the remnants of fuchsia lipstick colored her lips.

She peered through the smoke with narrowed eyes. "If you're selling anything, I'm not buying. Oh, a puppy. Come here, sweetheart."

I glanced at Mom and Shar. Sometimes, a dog was all a person needed to soften them up. I opened the back door and let Sheba out.

Tail wagging, she sat next to Carol who fished a peanut butter cracker from the pocket of her robe. "What do you gals want?"

"It's kind of a touchy subject. Mind if we sit?" I motioned to the steps and a couple of folding chairs.

"Suit yourself." She snuffed her cigarette out in an overflowing ashtray and lit another one.

"We're looking for a John Flamell and a Donald Wright." I sat on the steps leaving the chairs for the others.

"What do you want with those losers?"

"Flamell is missing, and Wright shot a police officer last night after a bar fight. The waitress told us the two men had fought a while back over you."

"Are y'all detectives?"

"Sort of," Mom said. "We're those people the police ask to help when they're short-handed."

Carol frowned. "I've heard of people like you from TV. You don't look like the type they usually ask for."

"That's what makes us perfect." Shar grinned. "Did you know Flamell was married?"

"Nope. He didn't act like he was and didn't wear a ring. That man was at Leroy's every night."

Which meant Carol was too.

She blew out a ring of smoke. "I have no idea where Flamell is, but Wright owns a chicken farm."

"We doubt he's there now. Any idea where he might hide out?" I leaned my elbows on my knees in order to see her face better. She didn't seem to be hiding anything, and most people's faces betrayed them when they lied.

"He goes hunting a lot and mentioned a cabin somewhere in the mountains near a lake. Since I'm not a fan of the outdoors, I didn't pay a lot of attention. If Flamell is missing, did you ask his wife where he was? I bet she kicked him out."

Having considered the same thing, I intended to question Margie again about whether she knew of her husband's wandering eye. "Not yet. We've learned that men often tell the girlfriend more than they tell their wife."

Her eyes widened. "I was never his girlfriend. We did nothing more than a bit of flirting at the bar and danced a time or two. One of our dances was what set Donald off. He said he didn't want to go to

Leroy's that night. We fought, and I went alone. Not with the intention of picking anyone up but to have a good time. He showed up, accused me of cheating, then started a fight with your missing man. The fight moved to the parking lot. I followed and went home, leaving them to their childish actions."

"Have you seen Wright since?"

"Of course. He came by here last night but left before I woke. He didn't say anything about a fight or shooting anyone. Who did he fight with?"

"A young man with a girl."

She shook her head. "Idiot. I didn't know he planned on going to Leroy's last night. He wasn't there when I was. My head starting aching, so I came home early. About eight o'clock, I think. He came by to check on me, so he said."

We'd just missed her. I handed her one of my business cards. "Please call us if you hear from him, but don't tip him off."

"You own a pet store? I'd like a dog."

"We don't have any right now, but if you keep an eye on the website, you'll know when we do." I smiled and thanked her for her time.

Back in the car, I turned to the others. "We didn't learn anything."

"Let's head out to that chicken farm," Mom said. "Maybe we'll find out more about the hunting cabin."

"We did learn that Carol wasn't having a fling with Flamell," Shar added. "And that Wright was there last night, which means he hasn't gone too far. It's only nine a.m. After the farm, we should visit

Margie again. She's hiding something from us."

A police car, siren wailing, sped past the trailer park. A unanimous decision to follow had us peeling away from Carol's trailer.

Traffic was stopped on the interstate. The squad car took the shoulder to somewhere down the line.

I put the car in park and stepped out, trying to peer over the other cars to see what had happened. "Looks like an accident."

"Let's go for a walk." Shar shoved her door open.

"We should stay here in case traffic starts moving again."

"I'm following the police."

I rolled my eyes and stayed by the car. "Relax. We'll know soon enough what happened. They'll start moving traffic soon."

"Fine." Shar plopped back in her seat and crossed her arms. "It could take hours."

Instead, we were moving at a snail's pace within fifteen minutes. I craned my neck to see what the holdup was. A large black truck had hit a tree head-on. No sign of the driver I could see. "That looks like Wright's truck."

"I bet he's headed on foot to the farm." Mom leaned on the front seat. "If we don't hurry, we'll miss him."

"I can't go anywhere, and put on your seatbelt. We'll go to the farm as soon as traffic is cleared." Then, I'd push the speed limit in hopes of spotting Wright.

Tapping the steering wheel with about as much patience as Barney, I contemplated our next move with Margie. The woman definitely had a secret. Instinct told me it had to do with her husband and the burglaries which had slowed with all the attention lately focused on Wright.

The slight glimpses of the thief though showed a smaller man. But the footprints pointed to Wright. Who was the smaller man, and how could Margie be connected, if at all?

Finally, traffic cleared enough for us to increase our speed and move around some of the slower moving vehicles. "Keep an eye out for Wright Farms."

Shar glanced at the GPS on her phone. "Take the next exit and head south. It looks as if his farm is down a dirt road. I pulled up a satellite image and there are three chicken houses plus a residence. I'd bet my favorite purse he's packing up to run right this second. A lot of forest surrounds his place. He won't be easy to find."

"If we can narrow down his location, McIlroy can take over. Send him a text about what we know."

Her fingers tapped away on the keyboard. "He replied that Wright is injured. Blood was found on the steering wheel of his truck. Consider him armed and dangerous." She laughed. "So are we."

"You didn't tell him that, did you?" I cut her a quick glance.

"Of course, I did. I don't want him to worry."

"He'll worry more knowing you're armed." I pressed the accelerator harder, parking half a mile from the chicken houses. "We walk from here. If we drive up, Wright will know we're coming, and I don't want him taking potshots at us from inside the house."

Come on, McIlroy. We might need you.

Chapter Thirteen

"Do not get into a shootout," I said. "Under no circumstances. I'm serious."

"This isn't the wild, wild west." Mom shot me that look most mothers are famous for. The one that said you're talking nonsense and should stop while you're ahead.

I wasn't one to follow a warning. "With you two, anything is possible."

After receiving glares from both Mom and Shar, I let Sheba out of the car and attached her leash to her collar. "Let's try to do this quietly."

"Gee, I thought we'd stomp through the woods like a bunch of first graders." Mom slung her purse over her shoulder and hitched up her chin.

"I suppose you let Alex know where we are?" Shar arched a brow.

"Of course, why?"

"Because he'll show up like a knight in shining armor and take all the glory after we do all the work."

What was wrong with these two? They acted as if everyone was against us, when in fact, it was the exact opposite. We were here merely to locate and observe, not take down the bad guy. I shook my head and led the way along the road's shoulder.

Thankful for a mild weather, I enjoyed the walk and the rustle of a breeze through trees just starting to turn to their autumn foliage. I didn't stop until the sign for Wright Farms came into view. Holding up my fist in the universal signal to stop, I peered around a large oak tree.

No vehicles were parked in front of a faded wooden house or by the three fairly modern chicken houses. Not hard to see where Wright's spent his money.

I put a finger to my lips, then waved the others forward. As we moved closer to the house, I noticed the front door open and jumped into the protection of the trees. It wouldn't help us any if we were spotted.

"Are we going in?" Mom asked. "Sneaking or knocking on the door like salesmen?"

"Wright will recognize me. We should circle around the back. Sheba will let us know if he takes off out the front."

"Then, you'll sic her on him, right?"

"In a matter of speaking." My dog would chase but not attack unless ordered by me. "Come on. Once we know for certain he's here, I'll send another text to McIlroy."

"He'd never reach us in time," Shar said. "Until a replacement for Rickson shows up, they're severely undermanned."

"There are two more officers." Although, I'd never met them. If I needed help, it was always the detective who showed up. "If we can safely contain Wright, we will." I didn't have a problem holding him as long as he didn't shoot at us. Not many people tried to get past Sheba once she cornered them.

We followed the tree line to the back of the house. A man's silhouette passed a window.

Adrenaline coursed through my veins. "Sheba and I will take the back. Mom, you and Shar go around front but stay out of sight. Call out that the police are here. If he runs your way, let me know, and I'll send Sheba to you." I started to sound like an experienced investigator. Television and life, I guess. After the mysteries I'd gotten involved in over most of the past year, my way of thinking had changed.

I still preferred running my store, but as long as Mom and Shar had the sleuthing bug, I'd be drawn in. When they headed to the front, I kept my eye on the back door and window. "Watch, Sheba."

Her ears perked up as she stood at attention.

"We've got you surrounded," Mom called from the other side of the house. "Come out with your hands up." Obviously, Mom watched more television than I did. Of course, lately, watching true crime took a back seat to living it.

As expected, Wright, gauze wrapped around his head, staggered out the back door. He took one look at me and my dog and limped toward the chicken houses. The car accident had slowed him down, allowing me and Sheba to follow at a fast clip rather than a sprint.

"Leave me alone." He glanced over his shoulder. "You've got nothing on me."

I glanced at a footprint he'd left in the dirt. Exactly like the one found at the scene of a B and E. "Pretty sure we do. Why not give yourself up? You're injured and need medical attention."

"Worry about yourself." He yanked open the door to the chicken house and disappeared inside.

I groaned. I hated chicken houses. The smell, the noise, not to mention feathers flying everywhere. "Stay focused, girl. No chasing the birds." I followed Wright inside as Mom and Shar rushed our way.

Wright was midway through the house. When I stepped inside, he shouted and waved his arms.

A cloud of squawking, panicked chickens surrounded me and Sheba. I shrieked and fended them off. Sheba cowered behind me. Through the haze of feathers and sawdust, Wright exited through a rear door.

"Why isn't your gun drawn?" Mom shoved a flapping bird away from her. "Menacing beasts."

"He isn't armed." I gave chase, doing my best not to trip over a feathered creature more frightened than they'd made me.

Outside, I glanced around, not seeing the man I sought. Groaning, I entered the next house, Mom and Shar close on my heels, only to again be swarmed by panicked chickens. "I can do this all day, Mr. Wright." No, I couldn't. I coughed, my lungs seizing. "Mom, am I allergic to chickens?"

"Looks that way. Your eyes are swelling."

Awesome. I rushed outside, taking a lungful of clean air. "You two go on without me. I'm going to lie down and die." I slumped against the building.

"I'm calling 911." Mom punched in the number, gave the state of our emergency, then resumed the chase with Shar, leaving me in a wheezing, huddled mess. What happened to her wanting to take care of me?

I made my way to the house and rinsed my face and exposed skin with an available water hose. Rinsing off the dust from the houses helped my breathing clear a bit. I washed my eyes again and blinked as Wright slipped into the woods. "Get him, girl." I released Sheba from her leash. She took off like a bullet.

"You look better," Mom said, joining me, "but you'll catch your death of cold being wet."

"Never mind that. We need to follow Sheba." I'd seek medical attention later if I worsened or was near death. Otherwise, fresh air and a change of clothes would suffice.

"You are a frail thing, aren't you?" Shar exhaled heavily. "Can't even go around a simple bird."

"Yes, I can." I glared. "Hundreds of them tell a different story." I followed Sheba, still struggling a bit to breathe.

"Should I be worried about you?" Mom asked.

"A little late for that now. I took care of the dust myself, thank you very much."

"Conserve your breath. Rest by that tree. Shar and I will flush him out and send him back your way."

What a great idea. I sat in a pile of pine needles at the base of a tree. "If I'm dead when you get back, I love you. Tell Dad."

"Don't be dramatic, sweetie." Mom and Shar resumed their chase, Mom casting one last glimpse over her shoulder before heading into the shadows.

Without my fur baby, loneliness assailed me. Normally, the woods soothed me with birds singing and trees whispering, but not with an injured madman out there somewhere. I pulled my gun from my waistband and set it in my lap, just in case.

From the trees came the occasional shout from Mom or Shar, crashing through underbrush, sounds that let me know the chase continued. I pulled my cell phone from my pocket and texted McIlroy about what was happening and that he might want to come before two of the Waterfall Sleuths did something foolish.

"Ten minutes away, at least," he responded. "Try to keep them under control."

Right. He gave me too much credit. Controlling Mom and Shar was harder than herding cats, and I'd tried both lately.

A loud crash to my right had me standing, hair on my arms standing at attention. "Mom?"

Wright stumbled into sight and collapsed at my feet. "Help me. I give up."

"My mother has that effect on people." I helped him to a sitting position and left him under Sheba's watchful eye while I resumed my seat a few feet away.

"Who's the guy who actually breaks into houses?" I tilted my head. "I know you're the one who makes sure the job gets done."

He shrugged. "They vary. Whoever the boss can find that's dumb or desperate enough."

"Who's the boss?"

"No idea." He closed his eyes.

"You're lying."

"Prove it."

Mom and Shar came into sight. "Oh, good. You got him." Mom grinned. "Good job, Trinity."

"He actually gave himself up."

"Probably the smartest thing he's ever done," Shar said. "Now spill your guts."

Wright leaned over and vomited.

"Gross. Not that way."

"I think he has a serious concussion," I said. "Running from you two didn't help him any."

Another crashing through the brush and Mom and Shar whipped around, guns at the ready. McIlroy froze. "Put those down. You could have shot someone."

"Sorry, darling." Shar smiled. "We got him for you."

McIlroy glanced at Wright. "I see that. Trinity, you look like—"

"Turns out I'm allergic to chickens."

He started to ask a question, then thought better of it and crouched next to Wright. "I'm taking you in, sir. Can you walk?"

"If we take it slow. And keep me away from those women."

McIlroy held out his hand and helped him to his feet. "I'll have an ambulance waiting near the house. Trinity, you need to be checked out, too."

For once, I wasn't going to argue.

We shuffled through the woods like a group of elderly people using walkers. A few times, Wright swayed, held upright by McIlroy.

"Are you the one who killed Mrs. Winston?" I asked.

"No."

"Were you involved in the dog-fighting ring?"

"Yes. Can you stop talking?"

"Are the burglaries to fund the fighting?" I wasn't going to stop questioning a suspect who had no chance of getting away.

"Yes."

"So, now that Jones is behind bars, who's running things now?"

"The same person responsible for the thefts. I already told you I don't know who it is."

"Don't you talk to them on the phone?" Why wasn't McIlroy asking anything?

"Yes, but their voice is computerized. I can't tell if it's a man or a woman."

As promised, an ambulance waited for us, and McIlroy turned Wright over to the capable hands of the paramedics. "Good questions, Trinity." He smiled.

"Why weren't you questioning him?"

"I prefer to do my interrogations at the station. You, as a civilian, don't have to abide by the fifth amendment. Once I get him there, I'll ask those same questions, so I can have them on record." He lowered his voice. "You might want to remind your mother that she now has a job. One she should actually show up to do."

I nodded and sat on the stoop of Wright's house, waiting for a paramedic to check on me. "I thought the fighting and the thefts might be connected. Now we have confirmation. The question now is...who is behind it all?"

"We're closer than we were yesterday." He clapped me on the shoulder. "We'll find them."

A rush of pride at the use of *we* flooded through me as a paramedic gave me a steroid shot and said I'd be fine by tomorrow. He told me to stay away from chicken houses, something I wouldn't have trouble doing.

"Well." Mom rubbed her hands together. "That was fun. What's next?"

Chapter Fourteen

The next two days passed in relative peace if you didn't count Mom and Shar, heads together when Mom wasn't working, as they tried to come up with a plan. Me? My job provided plenty of excitement, especially when I found a mixed-breed dog and her newborn puppies on the side of the highway. I brought them to the store and let the momma care for her babies in the pen usually occupied by Barney. He now had to stay with the daycare pets.

"Maybe after Wright's arrest, the others involved skipped town." Mom tossed her pencil on the table.

One could only hope. I glanced up from my computer. "We can assume you're correct if no more crimes occur."

"What if they're simply laying low for a while?" Shar sprang to her feet and opened the door for a grooming client. "Time will tell."

"Sitting around will drive me batty."

"Don't you have to be at work?" Since Mom started work at the station on Monday, I enjoyed a few hours without her moaning about lack of clues.

"Oh, shoot." She grabbed her purse and darted out the door.

"If Alex wasn't sweet on me, he might fire Lou. She hasn't proven to be very reliable." Shar led a shaggy poodle to the grooming room while I helped the dog's owner.

"Maybe I should buy one of those puppies for Robbie?" Heather said, picking up one of the pups from the pen.

"Take your pick. No charge."

"I'll wait until they're a little older. That gives me time to see which one fits better." She smiled. "I told David yes, and he agreed to give me a year before saying I do."

"That's wonderful."

"What about you and Brad?"

I shrugged. "We're not in any hurry." I had the feeling he might be, but I wasn't. Right now, I had the best of both worlds.

"Why are you so reluctant?" Heather sat down. "Your parents have a great marriage."

"I don't know. There's something that holds me back. Something that makes me afraid Brad will put a leash on me."

"He'd never do that."

My heart told me he wouldn't, but a niggle in my brain kept me from setting a date. I cupped my head in my hands. "I'm a mess."

She laughed. "Messes can be fixed. Why not

talk to your mom? She might be able to help."

"Ugh. She's in my business enough as it is. Oh, I almost forgot." She jumped to her feet and pulled a flier from her purse under the counter. "David and I are going to an escape room. Do you and Brad want to join us?"

"I've never done one before. That sounds like fun." I took the flier. "*Insane Asylum*? That sounds about right. I'll send him a text."

"No, the next one. It takes place outside. *Haunted Forest*." She tapped the paper.

"Creepy." I grinned and sent a text to Brad who replied almost immediately. "Sure."

"See y'all tomorrow night, then." Heather headed to the storage room.

I thought about what she'd said. Maybe I did need to talk to my mother about my marriage fears.

During her lunch break, Mom called. "This place is hopping. I can't go into detail because, well, you know, privacy and all, but I can tell you that Wright never did say he knew who he worked for or with."

"I'd have been surprised if he did."

"McIlroy has a new officer in his office. Name of Murphy. Older man. A bit of a grump."

"That's nice. That gives us three plus McIlroy." I half-listened as I paid invoices.

"Uh-huh, but something is up. McIlroy has been very secretive. He knows something but refuses to tell me."

"You answer the phone, Mom. You aren't law enforcement."

"Pooh. I work here, too, don't I? Gotta go. I'll

let you know if I hear anything pertinent to our investigation." Click.

I shook my head. What had McIlroy been thinking to hire my nosy mother?

"What did Lou say?" Shar leaned against the counter. "She promised to keep us apprised of any new developments."

"New police officer. Other than that, nothing."

"That isn't much help. Why haven't we spoken to Margie again? You know, about Carol?"

"She's been out of town on vacation according to the gossip mill at the salon." I'd overhead that tidbit while getting a trim. "I haven't forgotten. We can go after work. No more time off to go scouring the countryside. I pay you to be a groomer, not a detective."

She put a hand to her chest as if I'd wounded her. "You know I only go when I don't have clients. If you'd buy another van, I could ask questions and do my job."

"Okay. You're right. We'll look at vans after questioning Margie. I'm out of sorts today, and I apologize."

"No problem. Everyone is entitled to a bad day now and then." She smiled and headed back to the grooming station. Seconds later, a blast of water from the hose hit the window separating us.

I shrieked and slid back in my chair.

Shar's laughter pierced the glass.

Laughing, I shook my fist vowing revenge. I had the best friends who knew just how to get me out of a slump. I went back to work to the sound of a squeegee cleaning the window and pushed aside the fact our previous van had been blown to smithereens almost taking us with it.

"Time to close up." Shar pointed to the clock at exactly five. "Time's a wasting, and we have to pick up Lou."

"I'm coming. Sheba. Barney." I let the others out first and locked the door behind us, hoping Margie would be receptive to our visit, especially after her vacation.

As soon as Mom slid in the car, she started talking. "Another robbery last night that is being kept hush hush."

I stared. "Why and how do you know?"

"I saw the report. Here's the address." She handed me a post-it note. "Right next door to Margie Flamell. We can ask if she noticed anything." She lowered her voice to a whisper. "Another death."

"That's why the secrecy." Shar leaned forward. "If this spreads around, it could start a panic. Old women will be afraid to stay home alone. The store will run out of guns. We don't have enough officers to keep tabs on all of them. We should start patrolling at night."

I narrowed my eyes in the rearview mirror. "We will not. Didn't your home getting broke into cause you to think at all?"

"Danger comes with the job."

"This isn't our job."

"Since when did you become a scaredy-cat?"

"When someone tried to kill me." Ugh. I pulled away from the curb and headed to Margie's. Wasn't it enough I still went on their little escapades?

120

Imagine the trouble they'd get into if I didn't come along?

Not that I hated solving a mystery. I enjoyed bringing justice to the victims, but I'd reached the point where I liked to dig for information but pass it along to McIlroy. It seemed safer than confronting a suspect. Chasing down Wright could have ended very differently if he hadn't been injured in a car accident.

Maybe I *had* grown into a scaredy-cat. That wouldn't convince me to rush headlong into danger, though. For once in my life, I was the level-headed adult. I parked in front of Margie's house and waved as she stood from a rocking chair on her front porch.

"She doesn't look tanned," Mom said.

"Maybe she didn't go somewhere with lots of sun." I slid out, then opened the backdoor for the dogs.

"She doesn't look rested, either. Look at the shadows under her eyes."

"You can't see them from here."

"Oh, yes, I can." She slammed her car door.

Fine. I moved forward, stopping at the bottom step.

Margie's smile looked forced. "What brings y'all by?"

"This might touch on a nerve, but do you know a Carol Turner?" I asked.

"No, should I? Come sit down."

"We aren't staying long," Mom said. "We heard there was a robbery next door."

I cut her a sharp glance. "We'll get to that." I

turned back to Margie. "On the night of your husband's disappearance, he got into a fight with a Donald Wright over a woman named Carol."

"Really?" She fidgeted with a loose thread on the hem of her blouse. "Where was this?"

"Leroy's Bar."

"John did like that place, but I had no idea he was unfaithful."

"We don't think he was." I gave her a sympathetic look. "The trouble seems to have been with Wright. Are you sure you have no idea where your husband has gone?"

She gasped. "Please get your dog out of my roses." She rushed down the stairs, grabbing a rake. "Scram."

Barney gave up digging and faced the woman, his normal barks deeper and more menacing. The hair on his neck rose as he lunged toward Margie. Strange behavior for a dog so young.

I hurried to pull Barney back. "Naughty dog. I'm so sorry."

Margie quickly raked the mulch back into place. "If you feel the need to pay me a visit in the future, please leave the dogs in the car. I work hard on my plants. Why do you think I got rid of that dog?"

"I am so sorry." Barney tugged against his collar.

"I think y'all should leave now." Margie looked as if she wanted to hit me or the dog with the rake.

"What about your neighbor?" Shar asked.

"I don't know anything. I didn't hear anything. As for my husband, leave it be. He obviously didn't want to stay and has gone."

"You said he was dead." I studied her face.

"To me he is."

I dragged Barney back to the car, Sheba glanced back once before following. Her dark eyes focused on Margie who marched toward her porch, cell phone to her ear. "Well, that didn't go well." I shut Barney in the back of my SUV.

"Nope." Mom climbed into the front passenger seat. "We won't get anything more from Margie. Let's go next door."

Next door happened to be a quarter of a mile down the road. Crime scene tape fluttered from the wraparound porch. I guess when the houses were this far apart, the police weren't afraid of someone driving by and being able to tell a crime had taken place from the street. I drove up the long drive and parked.

"Do not enter the house." I shot them both a warning look. "We'll search the perimeter for clues, and that's it."

"What about the next-door neighbor?" Mom reached for her door handle. "They might know something."

"If this is supposed to be kept quiet, McIlroy won't like us questioning the neighbors. Let's see what we find here before doing anything else. Got it?"

"Got it." Mom exchanged a suspicious look with Shar.

Why did I feel as if I were babysitting a pair of rowdy toddlers? I let Sheba out of the vehicle but kept Barney safely inside so he couldn't get into trouble, wishing I could do the same with my mother and friend.

With Sheba padding by my side, I went around the corner of the house, studying the flowerbeds. Since the robber seemed to enjoy entering through windows, I felt it my best bet for finding footprints. With Wright in jail, I expected to find much smaller ones.

"Found a broken window," Shar's voice came from the other side of the house. "And footprints."

I darted around the next corner. Sure enough, a window just above my head had been broken. In the dirt around an evergreen bush was the faint impression of a shoe I guessed to be a size ten-and-a-half with an unoriginal zigzag pattern.

"Looks like the thefts have started back up for sure," Mom said.

"Right after Margie returned from vacation," Shar noted.

I widened my eyes at them. Coincidence? I started to think not. After all, Wright had said the automated voice he received on the phone calls could be either a man or a woman.

Why had she protected a rosebush going dormant during fall? I needed to take Barney back there when she wasn't home. If there were stolen goods buried, he'd dig them up for sure.

And just like that, I was fully moving ahead with snooping, right along with Mom and Shar. The familiar adrenaline rush that came when we were close to solving the mystery flooded through me.

Chapter Fifteen

"Want me to call Alex?" Shar stared at the footprint.

"No, that little orange flag tells me he already knows. Let's go shopping for a van so I can go home to have supper with Brad." I used my phone to take a photo of the print. "I want to return to Margie's after dark with Barney."

"Why?"

"She's buried something under her rosebush." I led the way back to the car and headed for the nearest car lot. I'd have to pretend to be taking the beagle for a walk, and he pulled away from me and started digging. The only answer I'd need was why walk the dog so far from my house or the penthouse? I'd worry about that if I needed to.

"I can't come," Shar said. "Alex is coming for supper."

"Your dad wants to go to the movies." Mom pouted.

"I'll take Brad."

"He isn't part of our club." Mom crossed her arms.

Rolling my eyes, I pulled away from the house. "I promise to let you know what we find."

"The van we purchase has to be like the last one." Shar headed across the car lot seconds after I turned off the engine.

"We'll have to buy a panel van and turn it into what you want," I said, hurrying to catch up.

"That'll take forever."

"No, it won't." I'd already spotted the perfect van. Plain white and waiting to be turned into something marvelous. "This one. With paint and our logo, it'll be perfect. I'll leave the inside up to you." Sliding the side door open, I checked inside. Perfectly empty. "Draw up your plans within the next day or two and I'll hire someone to make it the way you want. Your mobile business will be back up and running in no time."

A young man who didn't look old enough to be out of high school greeted us inside the showroom. "I have that same van used, if you want a lower price."

"How many miles?"

"Fifteen thousand. It used to be a rental. Want to take a look?"

"Anything that will save me money." I ignored Shar's frown. Why buy new when used was cheaper? Especially if it was just as good. I'd be writing the check after all.

The used van looked exactly the same as the new except for a couple of dings on the bumper.

"We'll take this one. Shar, want to drive it to the store?" I pulled out my checkbook.

"Yep. I'll be the one driving it every day." She took the keys offered by the salesman. "See you there. Lou?"

"I'll ride with my daughter. See you tomorrow."

As we drove home, I took the opportunity to ask Mom some questions about my hesitancy to get married. "Why do I feel this way?"

"Your grandparents, of course. Remember that summer you stayed with them when you were twelve?"

I scrunched my nose. "You'd think I'd remember more."

"My father, bless his soul, was an overbearing man who believed women should know their place and stay there. Why do you think I married your father? Because he was as different from my dad as a man could get. Your grandpa wanted the house spic and span at all times, and meals could not be late. Since you were female, he expected the same from you as he did your grandmother."

"She did seem quiet when he was around but smiled more and even laughed when it was just the two of us."

Mom put a hand on my arm. "Brad is nothing like your grandfather."

"He tries to boss me—" I grinned. "—but gives up."

"There you go. He's a smart one." She chuckled. "Why not wait a full year, then set a date? What's the rush? Although you are close to thirty."

"That's the same advice I gave Heather."

"Great minds think alike." She glanced in the sideview mirror. "I think we're being followed."

"What?" I glanced in the rearview mirror to see a battered green truck looming in the rear window. "Can you see Shar?"

"No. Maybe she's behind the truck." I called Shar on my car's Bluetooth. "Where are you?"

"Right behind the idiot driving up your tailpipe."

"Can you see who it is?"

"Only that they're wearing a baseball cap. I'll stay on their tail."

"Maybe they're just one of those people who follow too close." Mom turned in her seat.

"Or they intend to run us off the road." If they rammed the back of the vehicle, they could harm Barney. "Can you climb over and put Barney in the seat with Sheba? He'll be safer."

"Oh, Lord, don't let us get rammed when I'm not in a seatbelt." Mom clambered over. She quickly put Barney in the backseat and climbed in front. "This seems to happen to you a lot."

"No better place for an ambush than a long stretch of road." I pressed the accelerator.

Shar called. "I called in the license plate to Alex. The truck was reported stolen this morning. Alex said for you to get to the station as soon as possible."

"Working on it, thanks." I whipped down the next exit.

The truck followed, keeping consistent speed with me.

"Maybe he's trying to scare us," Mom said,

keeping her eyes on the truck.

"He's doing a good job." My heart threatened to beat free. Being chased down the interstate wasn't new; neither was getting run off the road, but I wouldn't call it one of my favorite things.

When I pulled into the police parking lot, the truck sped by. Shar stopped next to my vehicle and rolled down her window. "Want me to tell Alex we're here?"

"No. You can tell him I'm going to drop Mom off, then head to the penthouse. The truck left." Just a warning then. The unanswered question—why did he want to warn me?

"See you tomorrow."

I drove to the parking garage of the penthouse and took both dogs in the elevator to Brad's floor. After a kiss that dispelled any fear, I told him of our visit with Margie, her neighbor, and the drive home. "Will you go with me to Margie's after dark?"

He studied my face. "If you're going, I'm going. I feel better when you're with me than with Lou or Shar."

"I agree. What's for supper?"

"Filet mignon with blue cheese crust. I called room service." He removed his tie and tossed it on the back of a chair. "I've dealt with late deliveries all day and a broken popcorn machine. Movie goers get angry when there's no popcorn."

"Poor thing. That's part of the movie experience."

"My days are still more boring than yours. I'll change, so we can leave right after we eat."

I fed the dogs while I waited, my stomach

grumbling in anticipation of the upcoming meal. I glanced around the modern décor of the penthouse, surprised that I liked it almost as much as my mismatched eclectic style. Somehow, I'd find a way to blend the two when Brad and I were married.

"Room service."

I peered through the keyhole in the door to see a young man wearing the white and black of the complex's waiters. I opened the door and stepped back to let him in.

He wheeled a stainless-steel cart with covered dishes into the room. "The dining table?"

"Yes, please."

Sheba growled, putting herself between me and the waiter.

He jumped back. "What's with the dog?"

"Are you new?" I tilted my head. "I've never seen you here before."

"Yes. Today's my first day. I'll, uh, leave the cart for you." He rushed out the door.

Sheba refused to let me near the food.

"Move, girl." I tried to shove her away.

"Don't touch that." Brad stood in the doorway. "That young man does not work here." He grabbed his cell phone off the table and called McIlroy.

"You think it's poisoned?"

"Maybe."

"Darn. I'm starving." I fell into a kitchen chair, not surprised that our wonderful meal would go to waste because someone wanted me to stop nosing around.

"We'll pick up burgers on the way to Margie's."

I sighed and settled back to wait.

Half an hour later, a police officer wearing the badge of Murphy arrived to bag up the food. "Detective McIlroy warned me I'd see a lot of you."

"Welcome to Waterfall." I forced a smile.

"We'll send this to the lab and be on the lookout for the man matching the waiter's description."

"I'm betting he's also the one breaking into women's houses." He hadn't looked like a killer, but I'd been surprised before.

"I want to know how he entered a building with this type of security," Brad said, his face darkening. "The people who live here pay good money to be safe. This young man waltzed right up to the penthouse."

Murphy shrugged. "Maybe he paid off the doorman. It happens. We'll let you know what we find."

After the officer left, Brad clipped a leash on Barney. "Let's go talk to the doorman on our way out."

"Never saw anyone new," the doorman said. "Of course, I haven't been here long. Maybe try the kitchen?"

Brad nodded and headed that way, ignoring the protests about the dogs. "Who hired the new guy who brought up our room-service cart?"

"I did." The head chef approached us. "He arrived to work only a couple of hours ago. Was there something wrong with your meal, sir?"

"Yes, the police took it to check for poison. I need to know the man's identity."

"Follow me." The chef led us to a small office off the kitchen and opened a folder on his desk.

"Application says Mark Bayer." He turned the folder so we could see. "Is that him?" He tapped a photo.

"Yes." I'd bet Sheba's favorite toy that wasn't the man's real name. "I'm guessing he's gone?"

"Rushed out of here like his tail was on fire, muttering something about being sick to his stomach. Hard to find good help."

"May I have a copy of that application?" Brad asked.

"Absolutely, Mr. Armstrong." The chef hurried to make a photocopy. "I'm sorry about the night's events. May we make you another meal?"

"No, thank you. We're on our way out." With his hand on the small of my back, Brad rushed me to the garage and into his Mercedes. "I want to call McIlroy before we leave, although I don't think he'll have anything on Mark Bayer."

He called the detective, saying we'd drop off the man's application on our way to dinner, leaving out that we planned on stopping at Margie's. "No sense saying anything unless we find something," he said after he hung up.

"We might need a shovel."

"Sweetheart, I carry everything we need in my trunk. I have ever since you started getting involved." A dimple winked in his cheek. "You know what they say about being prepared."

I laughed. "I bet you were a boy scout."

"Guilty. Let's go see what Margie has buried under her rosebush."

Chapter Sixteen

A light shone in an upstairs window. Brad suggested we wait in the car until we knew for a fact Margie had gone to bed.

I glanced at my watch. Nine p.m. Shouldn't be too long now. Not if she was anything like my mother who snored by this time at night.

"You never told me about your trip to New York." I kept my gaze on the house, but my ears tuned to Brad. Usually, he told me all about his trips without me having to ask.

"I sold an office business to Valerie, thus dissolving any future partnership between us."

"You did?" I peered through the night, trying to judge from his expression how that made him feel. "Weren't you partners for a long time?" Not that it hurt my feelings at all. Whenever the gorgeous Valerie came up in conversation, a niggle of jealousy ate at me.

He reached over and took my hand. "I'm going

to focus my business around here from now on. This is where my life is. Here in Waterfall with you."

Tears pricked my eyes. "You really are the best," I said softly.

Brad leaned over to kiss me only to have his attention diverted as Margie's garage opened. "Guess we'll be able to search without her on the premises."

"Should we follow her?"

"No. We don't know how long she'll be gone and shouldn't waste this opportunity."

When her taillights turned out of sight, Brad opened his car door and grabbed Barney's leash. "No free run until we get closer, buddy."

"Wait. She's coming back." I grabbed Brad's arm and yanked him behind a bush.

"That isn't her."

A dark sedan turned off its lights before turning into the driveway and coasted toward the house. A couple of minutes later, what looked like a thin man from that distance approached the house.

"We need to get closer." I darted across the street and crouched behind a hedge in need of trimming. For someone who cared so much for her plants, Margie tended to neglect the larger ones. I parted the branches to see what the man was up to as Brad joined me.

"Don't run off like that again."

"Sorry," I whispered. "Can you see anything?"

"No. I could pretend to walk Barney past the house and see what the man does. Stay here with Sheba. Send her after me if anything goes wrong."

He stepped from our hiding place and strolled down the sidewalk, whistling.

Taking a bit more risk, I stood, just the top of my head showing above the hedge. Unless the stranger looked close, he might think my head was nothing more than tangled branches or a shadow.

The man froze behind one of the columns on the porch as Brad passed the house. Once Brad moved out of sight, the man reached for the front doorknob. Finding it locked, he jumped off the porch and headed toward the back.

"Come on, girl. We need to keep an eye on him." Staying as low as possible, I hurried after him.

What was he doing? Margie's house had already been broken into, or so she said. I started having my doubts the more I spoke to her. My gut told me the woman was right smack in the middle of what had been happening around town. Hopefully, tonight would fill in some of the blanks. I plastered my back against the wall and peered around the corner.

The stranger tried the back door, then stepped back and eyed an open second-floor window before grabbing hold of a trellis and starting to climb.

I stifled a scream as someone touched me. "Brad, you scared an hour off my life."

"What happened to not running off?" He hissed.

"I couldn't let him get away." I glanced around again to see the man's leg slide through the window. "He's inside."

Barney chose that minute to start barking.

The man's second leg froze halfway through the open window, then inched inside.

"Shh." Brad put his hand around the dog's muzzle.

"I could climb that." I studied the trellis.

"And have that man waiting to clonk you? No way."

"We need to know what he's looking for."

Headlights broke through the night, drawing our attention back to the front of the house. Margie had returned home.

"Should we warn her?"

"Wait." Brad pulled me out of sight as Margie exited her car and circled the other vehicle. "She doesn't seem alarmed."

"A meeting she forgot about?"

"Maybe." He pulled me back to the hedge.

Margie climbed the porch and unlocked the front door yelling at someone named Sam. "I know you're in here. You could have waited for me." She slammed the door behind her.

"Can we try peeking through a window?" I made a move forward.

"Barney will give us away. Maybe she'll leave again." He put a hand on the dog's head when he started to bark.

"Where's the remote to his collar?"

"I left it at home." He picked the dog up.

Sheba managed to poke her big head through the hedge. Unfortunately, she couldn't tell us what she saw, heard, or suspected. I hated waiting.

What seemed like forever but was likely only a few minutes, the front door opened and the man came out. He said something to Margie who slammed the door in his face. He got in his car and drove away. The lights in the house flickered out.

After another fifteen minutes of no activity, Brad stepped from hiding and had me show him the rosebush in question. He unhooked the leash from Barney who immediately started digging.

"Watch the house, Sheba." I jumped out of the way of flying dirt, knowing my girl would let us know if someone came.

"Is that a hand?" I clapped my hand over my mouth. It was.

"It's time to call McIlroy." Brad clipped the leash back on Barney and pulled him back.

Sheba growled.

"I told you to keep that dog away."

I turned and stared at the gun in Margie's hand. "Sorry. I'm not good at following orders. I assume we found your husband?"

"What?" She tried and failed to act surprised.

"There." I pointed at the hole, keeping her distracted long enough for Brad to send a text to the detective.

"Poor Joe." The hard tone in her voice belied the words.

"You're a horrible actor, Margie." I crossed my arms. "You've been found out."

"Nope. Move to that little trapdoor at the back of the house. Now."

Brad reached around him.

"Grab that gun and I'll shoot your girlfriend, then your dog." Margie waved the gun. "Turn around, put your hands on top of your head, and I'll relieve you of the temptation to do something stupid."

Sheba moved forward.

Margie trained the gun on her. "Call her off. I have no beef with this dog."

"Down, Sheba." I snapped my fingers for her to come to my side.

"I'm not going to tell you to get in the cellar again. Now, go."

We went.

Brad opened the cellar door and headed down first, turning to help me down the stairs. "Now what?"

"I'm going to go in my house, shed a few tears at having to set it on fire, and leave the lot of you to burn." She slammed the cellar door. A bolt slid into place.

"Too bad the floor isn't dirt," I said. "Barney could dig us out. Did you send the text?"

"I'm not sure." Brad held up his phone. "No service in here, so I'm hoping it went through before she locked us in."

"There has to be a way out of here. Most cellars have an entrance to the inside of the house, don't they?"

"Maybe." Brad turned on the flashlight feature of his phone and shined it around the walls. "I'm guessing she's out there digging up the body to hide it somewhere else."

"Or putting it in the house she plans on burning down." What was one more burned corpse added to ours? I glanced at my phone. No service either. Could McIlroy track us if we didn't have service? If Brad's text didn't go through, he wouldn't know we were missing. Shar and my parents knew I was having supper with Brad. No one would look for us until morning. By then it would be too late.

My breath came in gasps. I bent over to control the fear that washed over me as a wisp of smoke came from behind shelves holding canned goods. Wait. I straightened. Smoke from the wall meant an opening. "Brad, over here."

I started knocking jars and cans off the shelves. Glass shattered on the concrete floor.

The dogs yelped and cowered in a far corner.

My efforts uncovered a vent. "I think I can squeeze through there. It must come out in the house, right?"

"In theory." He yanked the vent cover off. "It's tight and dark. Are you sure?"

"There's no other way. If I can wiggle out, I can remove the board from the cellar door and get you and the dogs out." Otherwise, the cellar would fill with smoke and we'd die of asphyxiation. Not the way I wanted to go.

He pulled me to him and gave me a hard kiss. "Be careful. I love you," he said, his voice husky.

"I love you too." I caressed his cheek, then turned on the flashlight on my phone and climbed into the vent on my stomach. Tight, dark, with dank dirt. Please don't fall in on me.

Sheba whined behind me.

"I'll hold her back," Brad said.

Good. My dog would never fit. Please, God, don't let me get stuck.

The further I went, the narrower the crawl through. As small I was, I wouldn't make it. I shimmied backward until I was once again in the cellar. "Sorry." I leaned into Brad.

"It's okay." He pulled me to a sitting position. A haze of smoke hovered above our heads.

The dogs came to us, laying their heads in our laps, providing what comfort they could under the circumstances.

I coughed. My eyes watered, then I stretched out on the floor, prolonging breathing for as long as possible.

Brad lay beside me, wrapping his arms around me. My breathing matched his, in and out, in and out. If I had to die, then there could be no better place than wrapped in his arms.

The cellar door opened. We jumped to our feet.

"You okay in there?" McIlroy peered down at us.

"Better now." Brad led me from the cellar.

"Sorry. Today's my day off. I was sleeping and didn't check my phone until I got up to use the bathroom. A neighbor called in about a fire. After your text, I assumed the worst."

"Oh, sweetie." Shar rushed forward and wrapped me in a hug. "They found a decomposing body inside the front door."

"Joe Flamell, we think." I smiled up at her. "You're a wonderful sight."

"I had to come after knowing you might be in trouble. The fire department is putting out the fire. It hadn't spread past the kitchen yet."

"Any sign of Margie?"

She shook her head. "Gone."

I explained to her and McIlroy about the stranger we'd seen and Margie locking us in the cellar. "She called him Sam."

"Could you pick him out if you saw him again?" McIlroy asked.

I shrugged. "It's dark."

Brad shook his head. "Slim, Caucasian, about five-ten. Drives a dark sedan. That's all I could tell, but here's the driver's license." He pulled up a note on his phone. "Typed it in when I walked Barney past the house."

The detective copied it onto a pad of paper. "Might give us something. Y'all need to be checked out by the medics?"

"No," I said. "The smoke hadn't gotten too bad."

"Why are you covered in dirt?" Shar tilted her head.

"I tried to crawl through a tunnel. It was too narrow, even for me."

"At least you tried." She patted my shoulder. "Wait until your mother hears about this. Now, all we have to do is find this Sam guy and Margie to put this case to rest."

McIlroy groaned.

Chapter Seventeen

"I've never been to an escape room before," David said at supper that night. "Especially one outside. Could be kind of creepy." He waggled his eyebrows.

More than ready for some fun after being locked in Margie's cellar, I nodded. "I've not been to one, either. It's something new around here, isn't it?"

"Little Rock has one, I think." Brad wiped his mouth with his napkin. "At least it isn't cold yet. We've had a mild fall so far."

I finished off my burger, sliding my leftover fries to Brad who smiled. "The body in Margie's house has been identified as her husband. She is now officially the top suspect in a murder case."

Heather groaned. "No mystery talk tonight. I don't get a night away from Robbie very often. Let's keep it fun."

I laughed. "Mom would consider this type of conversation as fun." After getting over the shock that someone had tried to burn me alive, Mom pouted about missing out on the excitement, stating she would never have willingly gone into the cellar. She'd have taken the bullet.

No amount of arguing about every breath meaning an opportunity of escape could convince her otherwise. I was relieved she hadn't been with us. "Let's go escape the haunted woods." I stood.

Brad drove to a cabin down a dirt road with a canopy of autumn foliage over us. A slight breeze whispered through the trees, adding to the night's ambiance.

A young man in a plaid shirt and overalls greeted us on the porch. "Welcome. You'll go through the cabin first where you will find yourselves locked in with a madman. You must escape the cabin, then flee into the woods."

"Been there, done that," I muttered.

"You may touch everything. If it's attached to the wall or floor, please do not attempt to pull it free. Look for a key."

"Will there really be someone in there with us?" Heather asked, moving closer to David's side. "Because I've been chased through the woods before by a crazy person."

"These are all actors here." The man picked up an axe leaning against the cabin wall. "I will be inside, but you'll rarely see me. Just know that I am there. In the woods will be others waiting to make your escape difficult. Because this is an outdoor adventure, you have two hours to find your way out. Climbing through the barbed wire fence is prohibited. It's private property and not ours." He handed me an electronic tablet and each of us flashlights. "Place your cell phones in that bucket by the door. The countdown is on here. You may ask for clues, but each clue you use will erase five minutes of your time. If you give up, just give a shout and someone will come rescue you. You're searching for a red gate. Ready?"

"Absolutely." Since our night of fun resembled past reality, I felt certain we'd find our way out in record time. I hugged the tablet to my chest and followed the others into the cabin.

The door slammed shut behind us. David reached for the knob. "Locked."

"Of course, it is. Wouldn't be hard to find our way out if it wasn't." Heather stood in the middle of the front room.

I joined her, noting worn plaid furniture, a scarred coffee table, a small kitchenette with a table, and two doors at the opposite end. "I'll look for the back door; y'all search for the key." I opened the first door to reveal a small bathroom barely bigger than a closet. The second door revealed a bedroom with no back door. Maybe we were to go back out the front? That didn't make sense. And where was the axe-wielding young man? The cabin didn't hold many hiding places.

Speaking of…he banged on the window, leering at me through the glass. I yelped and returned to the others. "When we get out, we'll have to sneak past the Axe Man. I didn't find another door."

"A window." David pointed to a lock on a side window. "Going to be a tight fit for me and Brad."

"Heather and I will go out and open the front

door. Find the key?"

"No, but we found a clue." Brad shined a flashlight on the front of the refrigerator. Illuminated in the beam was "350."

"The oven." I opened the oven only to find it empty, so I turned the knob, tapping my foot as it preheated. Finally, a beep and a small drawer opened in the wall above the stove. Inside was another clue. "Good grief. We've been in here twenty minutes already." I handed the clue to Brad.

"Having a bad hair day?" He read. "That's odd."

"There's a mirror in the bathroom." I headed that way and opened the medicine cabinet. Empty. "Ah." I turned on a hair dryer. Nothing.

"Here." David took the dryer and removed the filter. "Bingo." He held up a key.

"Well, that wasn't too hard," Heather said, grinning. "Let's climb out that window."

I had a feeling the hardest part was yet to come. When I went to unlock the window, Axe Man appeared, tapping the head of his weapon on the glass. "Someone needs to distract him."

"By trying to get out another window?" Brad glanced toward the bedroom. "We'll try that. Come on, David."

"That axe looked real." Heather paled.

"They aren't allowed to touch us."

"What if they don't know that? I read a book once where a gal got chased through a funhouse by an axe-wielding clown."

I shuddered. "Stop it." I put the key in the lock the second the man rushed toward the back of the house.

"Doesn't this seem too easy? I mean, we found the way out in half an hour."

"The woods will be harder. We won't know which way to go." I slid the window open and stuck out my head. "Coast is clear."

From the bedroom came banging and yelling.

I climbed through, Heather right behind me. We darted to the front. I removed the plank barring the door. "Hurry."

David and Brad thundered from the house. Brad grabbed my hand, David taking Heather's, and we sprinted for the woods.

"Which way?" David asked.

I shrugged. "Guess we go until we see someone chasing us, then go the opposite way?"

"They might steer us wrong," Brad said. "The goal is to keep us from reaching the gate."

"Right." I stared at the path stretching in front of us. "So, this is probably a decoy." I studied the area. "Look. There's a faint arrow on this rock." Barely discernible in the dark, a tan arrow pointed to our right.

"Good eye." Brad clicked off his flashlight. "Lights off. Maybe it will take them longer to find us."

Adrenaline coursed through me. Being chased was a lot of fun when it wasn't real.

Maybe fifty yards into the woods, we found a man in camouflage fatigues slumped against a tree. "Nice touch." I motioned to the blood on his head.

Brad leaned closer. "It might be real."

My heart dropped to my knees. "Do you think he ran into a low branch?" Please, be just an accident.

After checking for a pulse, Brad shook his head. "Things just turned very real."

Heather's eyes widened in the moonlight. "You mean…"

"Is this what happens to y'all on a regular basis?" David leaned against a tree.

"Who, other than my parents, knew we were coming to the haunted forest?"

He cleared his throat. "I might have mentioned it to a few people on my rounds."

"Margie Flamell, for one?"

He nodded.

"Oh no." Heather clutched his arm. "We're out here with a real bad guy."

Why couldn't I have one night of fun without running for my life? "We don't know that for sure."

From out left came a shout, then nothing. I swallowed against the boulder in my throat and pulled up a hint from the tablet. "Doesn't say anything about an unconscious man. The next hint is to follow the moon's path."

"What if there isn't a moon?" Heather asked.

"Come on." Brad took my hand again. "Look how the trees have been trimmed through here, allowing some light in. We go this way. If we find the barbed wire, we'll follow it to the gate. Try to be as quiet as possible."

"Y'all can keep your mystery-solving," David whispered. "I'll stick to deliveries."

"My sentiment exactly." Heather hugged his arm.

"Shh." I glanced over my shoulder.

A shot rang out. The bullet slammed into a tree. Definitely not part of the game.

Brad pulled me off the path and into thicker brush. "We need to find our host. He can call the police."

"If he hasn't been knocked out," I said.

Brad once again reminded us not to talk, then hunched over, and moved slowly through the woods, the rest of us following so close it was a wonder we didn't trip over each other.

We found another unconscious man near the bank of a small stream. I couldn't see Margie being able to take them out. She had to have help. The skinny robber? How many were out here not part of the game?

"Whatever happens, stay together," Brad whispered.

I intended to, keeping a firm grip on his hand. "Since we're not playing the game anymore, should I ask for another clue?"

"Wouldn't hurt."

I let go of his hand and pressed the clue button. "The music of a babbling brook covers all sound. That means we should head away from the creek."

Another gun shot rang out. We scattered.

I ducked behind a rotting log. "Brad?" Couldn't hear a thing over the creek. Who invented this stupid game?

Someone whispered my name. Knowing Brad wouldn't be far and would never leave me, I headed toward the sound. It didn't take long for me to figure out the whisper had been nothing but wishful thinking. I stopped and tried to listen past the sounds of an autumn forest.

Leaves crunched. Friend or foe? Dare I risk exposure to find out? What if Brad or one of my friends was being hit over the head? My breathing accelerated. Calm down. You're no good to anyone if you pass out. "Brad?"

Not hearing anything more, I risked standing and darted from tree to tree in an attempt to stay hidden. I was bound to run across someone sooner or later. Hopefully it would be Brad. If Sheba were here, we'd already be rid of this place. If Barney was here, he'd dig us out.

I found Axe Man dead from the very axe he'd carried. Hopefully, he put up one heck of a fight. I blinked back a shudder and pulled up another clue. "Give it to me in plain English, please." I glanced at the screen. "The sun rises in the morning."

No, duh. Which way was east? Stupid tablet. Stupid game.

I took a deep breath and headed back to the creek. It would lead me to the fence. I'd take my chances following it until I reached the gate, then I'd hide and wait for the others to join me.

A gunshot spurred a faster pace. I couldn't tell which direction it had come from, but since it didn't hit me, a tree, or the ground at my feet, I didn't think I was the target. Please, God, let the others find their way.

The tablet started ticking like a bomb, the loud noise pinpointing my location as effectively as a flare. I dropped it and took off running.

Chapter Eighteen

Someone grabbed me and tackled me to the ground, clamping a hand over my mouth. I peered up into Brad's face. "Oh, my gosh." I wrapped my arms around his neck and kissed him. "I've never been more scared in my life."

"We aren't out of the woods yet, sweetheart." He pulled me to my feet. "No pun intended."

"How did you find me?"

"That stupid ticking tablet. Then, I followed the sounds of a mad dash through the forest. You weren't exactly subtle."

Which meant the bad guys knew where we were. "All I could think about was getting away from the ticking. Have you seen David and Heather?"

He shook his head. "Let's find that gate."

We slid down an embankment to follow the creek and found Heather cowering under an overhang. Tears marred her face. "I lost David and my flashlight."

"Stay with us. We'll find him." I hoped, not knowing how much of an outdoorsman he was. "Any sign of strangers?"

"I heard some footsteps while I was hiding but didn't dare come out to see who it was. Can't we stay here? Eventually, we'll be missed. Someone will come for us. Thanks to David, most of Waterfall knows we went to the Haunted Forest."

"They won't miss us until morning." I hugged her. "Come on."

Brad scoped out the area, then waved us forward. "Stay close. Stay quiet. Hold onto each other."

"I'm not leaving without David." Heather refused to budge.

"What if he's already found the gate and is waiting for us?" I gripped her arm. "Staying in one place will get us killed. Think of Robbie. Your son needs his mother."

"All right."

We continued to follow the creek until it wound away from the direction Brad insisted was east. When this was all over, I would insist Brad take me on a vacation. Somewhere far enough away that we could have fun without running for our lives. Somewhere with a beach where I could see for miles in every direction.

"I see the gate." Brad grinned over his shoulder. "Let's make a run for it."

"David." Heather moved what I thought was a pile of leaves. "I recognized his cologne."

He opened his eyes. "I've been shot."

"How bad?" Brad helped clear away the leaves.

"Just a graze in the arm, I think, but it hurts like the dickens. I tore off one of my sleeves and bandaged it, then hid, knowing y'all would come this way eventually." He sat up. "I found the gate but couldn't leave without Heather."

"I felt the same way." She cupped his face. "Let's go home."

We dashed for the gate, skidding to a halt as Margie, flanked by two gun-wielding men, stood on the other side of our goal.

"This is fun." She grinned. "Let's play some more. In order to make things fair, we'll open this gate and give you a ten-minute head start. Then, we'll pick you off one by one, saving the nosy pet-store owner for last." She glanced at David. "Winged you, I see. I do want to thank you for letting us know your plans. It sparked a great idea in my head, didn't it?"

"You're out-of-your-mind nuts." I glared at her, my hands curled into fists.

One of the men opened the gate. "Your ten minutes starts now."

Holding my hand, Brad sprinted through the gate and into a forest thicker than the one we'd paid to play in. "Anyone know this area?"

"No," we said in unison.

"No tablet to give us clues this time," I said. Finding our way out would be a lot more difficult.

"We go as fast as we can, not stopping until we reach a road or a house, unless David needs a break or it's time to be quiet."

"I'm good, man. Don't stop on my account. I'll

run until I die if I have to."

"In Trinity's world, you just might," Heather said. "This is why I haven't joined their stupid club. I enjoy living too much."

Brad increased our speed, making speech impossible. Soon, the only sounds were our raspy breathing and pounding feet. He glanced at his watch. "Seven minutes gone. We slow down and go more quietly now. No talking. Watch every placement of your feet so a snapping twig doesn't give us away. Take two minutes to rest, then we move on."

I leaned against a tree, afraid that if I sat I'd never get up. Clouds moved in, obscuring the moon. Good. It would provide us a bit of protection even if it made our flight more difficult. We could do this. I'd been in tight spots before and came out fine. Keeping my ears trained on any sound not made by the woods, I stayed close to Brad's side as he led us on. No way would I allow us to be separated again, not even if a bullet landed at my feet.

From the expressions on the faces of the others, they were having the same thought.

My lungs struggled to draw in air, and my legs burned. I resolved again to start going back to the gym and meant it this time.

No sounds of pursuit reached my ears. How could Margie and her goons move so quietly? Being careful had slowed us down considerably.

I glanced overhead as the clouds moved away from the moon, allowing a brief glance of our surroundings before drifting back across the shining orb. Leaves rained down on us, carpeting the ground with crunchiness. No matter how hard I tried, I couldn't avoid stepping on them.

Brad held up a closed fist, calling a halt, then led us to the left. I tried to hear what had alerted him but couldn't hear past the sound of my breathing. I glanced back to see David falter, then catch himself on the trunk of a tree.

"We need to take a break," I whispered.

"Can't." Brad pushed forward.

"But, David—"

"I'm fine," He said hoarsely. "I'd rather struggle on than stop and be killed."

Good point. I forced myself to take another step, then another.

A strong thirst consumed me. My stomach, not used to being up so late, complained, thinking it was time for breakfast. It couldn't be later than eleven. A quick glance at my watch confirmed the time.

My mind whirled with ridiculous thoughts. I didn't mind. Those thoughts, silly as they might be, helped keep me from falling into panic.

A muffled word. The snap of a twig. We ducked and froze.

"They're smarter than we thought," a man said. "Marg said there wasn't a whole brain among the lot of them."

"She's been wrong about a lot of things. Dude, you killed an old woman. If we're caught, we'll be locked up for the rest of our life."

"What do you want to do?"

"Make a run for it. Go to Oklahoma or North. Somewhere nobody knows us. Let Margie deal with the aftermath herself. I ain't killing nobody else for no amount of money."

"Let's do it."

Sounds of retreat had me releasing the breath I'd held. "Should we follow?"

Brad nodded. "They'll know the way out of here."

Not caring where Margie was hiding, if she was even out here, I stayed close on Brad's heels. I suspected she hired those men to do her dirty work and waited somewhere in relative comfort for them to catch us.

Eventually, we stepped out of the trees onto an old logging road that didn't look as if it had been used in a long time. Brad stayed close to the tree line and led us back the way we'd come. "If we can reach the gate, then the cabin, we'll have our car and can hightail it out of here."

I liked that plan.

We made it back within an hour. The penthouse in another half hour where we all crashed until nine a.m.

The aroma of cooking bacon roused me from my sleep. I tossed off the afghan I'd covered with on the sofa and padded to the kitchen. "Smells wonderful."

Brad turned from the stove. "I called McIlroy. He should be here soon."

"Great. We can relive that nightmare telling him all about it." I took a seat on a barstool at the kitchen island. "Heather and David still sleeping?"

"Yes. She called the babysitter last night and said she'd pick up her son this morning." He stepped over and kissed my neck. "You were great last night."

"By not dying?" I smiled.

"Yep." He winked and returned to the stove.

By the time the omelets were finished, Heather and David joined us in the kitchen. "That guestroom bed is the most comfortable thing I've ever slept on," Heather said.

"Glad you slept well." Brad set a plate in front of her. "David, you need medical attention today."

He nodded. "Way too tired last night. Arm hurts, but bleeding stopped."

A knock sounded at the door.

Heather shrieked and paled.

"It's just the detective." I went to the foyer and peered through the peephole before opening the door.

"You can't go on a simple date without getting into trouble, can you?" McIlroy shook his head.

"Just the way my luck goes, I guess." I closed and relocked the door. Even with the apartment complex's tight security, I wasn't taking any chances. Bad guys had infiltrated the place before. Of course, one had been a dirty cop we'd trusted.

"Officers are scouring the woods for the dead guy and the identities of the wounded. The phone has been ringing off the hook asking for help. The ones who weren't killed are holed up in the cabin of the escape room. You four were lucky."

"The two men with Margie were fleeing," I said. "We have no idea what happened to her."

"Then, that means she's most likely still around. You'll need to be careful." He glanced at Brad.

"Ever considered putting your girlfriend on a leash?"

"I have. Breakfast?" He held out a plate.

"No, I'm too busy. Shar is champing at the bit to hear all about the latest adventure at work today. Said she had a great sense of direction and could have found the way out in a short amount of time." He grinned.

"Sure." I laughed and cut into my cheddar and bacon omelet. My mother would want to know all the details, too. "Heather, take the day off. Spend it with Robbie."

"Are you sure?"

"Yep, I'll be fielding questions all day once news of this gets out. Could you have one of your officers bring us our phones? They're in a basket in the cabin."

McIlroy headed to the door. "Sure, I'll bring them by the store as soon as I have them. I'll keep you posted." He left, Brad locking the door behind him.

When I arrived at the store, Shar had already opened and was grooming Greta, Mrs. Nelson's schnauzer. She waved me to the next room. "Tell."

I propped on a stool and recounted the previous night's events. "Mom at work?"

"Yes, I'm sure she'll dig as much out of the officers as she can before coming here on her lunch break." She towel dried the dog. "How would the escape room have been if not changed by a demented woman?"

"Fun, probably. Getting out of the cabin was easy, if not creepy. The woods was another story." I shuddered. "Maybe the creepy came from how real it was."

"How real it turned out to be, you mean."

"Yeah. Doubt I'll want to do that again any time soon."

She turned on the hair dryer, leaving me to check emails. Before I'd booted up my computer, a customer arrived.

She handed me a sheet of paper. "This was taped to the front window." The woman glanced around the store. "I need some dog food for a pup with a sensitive stomach."

I directed her toward an expensive but healthy alternative to what she'd been using and read the note.

Our game is not over.

Chapter Nineteen

Shar peered over my shoulder, having snuck up on me as I sat in dread. "That woman is pure evil."

"I haven't done a thing to her but try and help her find her missing items."

"Found her dead husband." She patted me on the shoulder. "Shut down the dog ring. Locked up her top henchman."

"But I didn't do any of those things until you and Mom roped me into them." I set the note aside to give to the authorities. "I'm glad she isn't after one of you, but seriously—"

"It ought to make you feel good, in a weird way, that Margie considers you a threat." She headed to the door to assist a customer arriving with a standard poodle.

I sent a text to McIlroy, then could almost hear him groan in his return text that he'd come by within the hour. While I waited, I thought back over my encounters with Margie and couldn't come up with a single reason why she wanted me dead. Maybe it was simply because I'd been the sole cause of her loss of income.

Rather than a victim of a theft, she'd been the perpetrator. Why kill her husband though? She'd said she hadn't known about his infidelities. Was she lying? Was Carol Turner in danger?

My first reaction was to grab my car keys and check on her. After last night's romp through the forest, I felt it prudent to wait until after work when someone, preferably Brad, could go with me. What if waiting was too late for Carol? I couldn't wait.

"Come, Sheba. Shar, hold down the fort. I'll be back."

"Where are you going?"

"To check on Carol Turner. Tell McIlroy when he arrives the note is on my desk."

In the car, I made sure my gun was in the glove compartment, Sheba secure on the front seat, then we headed back to the trailer park. Carol's trailer didn't look as if anyone had been there in days. Still, I had to check. I took my gun and exited the car, leaving Sheba to follow.

The ashtray on the small table by the front door overflowed with cigarette butts. Dead flies floated in a half empty glass of soda. I climbed the three cement steps and pushed open a door not fully closed. "Carol? It's Trinity Ashford."

Sheba whimpered and nudged my leg. Her reaction to stepping into the trailer caused the hair on my arms to rise.

"Carol?" Sweat beaded on my upper lip. The

closer I got to the bedroom, the stronger the smell I'd had the displeasure of encountering before. I knew before pushing open the door at the end of the hall what I would find.

The woman lay on her bed, a bullet hole between her eyes. Dried blood stained the pillow under her head. It looked as if someone had shot her in her sleep.

I dialed McIlroy.

"I said I'd be there in a few."

"Change of plans," I said. "I'm in Carol Turner's trailer. She's dead. Looks like for a couple of days at least."

"Get out of there. Lock yourself in your car. I'm on my way." Click.

No problem. I rushed back outside, took huge gulps of fresh air, and slipped back into my car. I locked the doors and slouched down in my seat before calling Brad.

"Do you want me to come?" He asked after I told him what happened.

"No, McIlroy should be here soon."

"You shouldn't have gone alone."

"I did give it a second thought, but I wasn't sure how much time she had." Poor thing. All she wanted was to have fun and enjoy what beauty she had left.

"The car is more exposed than the trailer would be."

"True, but there's a decomposing body in there. How's your day going?" Mundane questions would help distract me.

"Not too bad so far. Had an usher quit, but

there's a waiting list of high schoolers wanting a job. The position will be filled by tonight. I purchased a few empty storefronts off Main Street. I'll renovate them and see about renting them out."

"You're serious about focusing your business here."

"Yes. This is where I want to be."

I smiled, knowing I was the major reason he stayed, leaving city life behind and embracing the small-town way. "I'll see you after work."

Another fifteen minutes and the detective pulled behind my car. I stepped out and glared at him. "What took you so long? I could have been abducted." Regret filled me at the exhaustion on his face.

"We had a lead on those two men in the woods last night but lost it as they crossed the state line. I've alerted the authorities in Missouri to be on the lookout. Stay here." He turned and entered the trailer, exiting a few minutes later. "Did you touch anything?"

"Just the door handle." There'd been no need to check for a pulse. "Any sign of Margie?"

"No, but I'm sure she isn't far. Go back to the store. I'll pick up the note later. Be careful, Trinity. Don't dawdle. Stay alert."

I nodded and headed back to work where I recounted finding Carol to Shar. "Margie will come for me next."

"Stay in the penthouse with Brad. Don't be alone in your apartment."

I petted Trashcan who leaped onto my lap. "I will, but I hate leaving these two guys alone all the time."

"You're with them all day most days. They hang out in the store during the day. They're fine." She narrowed her eyes. "But you aren't. Maybe the Waterfall Sleuths isn't a good idea."

"We did solve the crimes, though. I'm thinking that instead of resisting like I did this time, I might as well charge into the mysteries. The bad guys seem to challenge me despite my wanting to stay out of things."

"We should take self-defense classes." She plopped a flier on the counter. "Tonight at the gym. I've already told Lou."

Learning some moves wouldn't stop a bullet, but it might help keep me from being kidnapped if I could get close enough to the one intent on taking me. It was something I'd been meaning to do. "I'm in."

Since the class started at five, I closed shop early, leaving my pets free to roam between the apartment and the store, and headed next door with Shar. Mom, dressed in hot pink leggings and an oversized shirt in the same color, waited outside.

"You look like a highlighter," I said.

She eyed my jeans. "How are you going to kick in those?"

"I have a locker here with workout clothes. I'll change."

"Better hurry. You're going to be late for class." She frowned and entered the gym.

Since Shar wasn't dressed appropriately either, she followed me. We changed quickly and were only five minutes late. Not bad, but I ducked my head to avoid the stern gaze of the instructor.

"Since some people don't seem to respect time, I'll take one of them as volunteer. You." She pointed to me. "What's your name?"

"Trinity Ashford." I sighed and moved to the center of the mat. "You?"

"Alice. You may call me Instructor. Now, pay attention. If I were to grab you from behind like this, what would you do?" She put a choke hold on me.

Putting my hands between Alice's hands and my neck, I squatted, turning my head toward Alice and my left leg behind her. I grabbed behind her knees when her hold loosened. She fell backward. I slipped free and grinned.

"Where did you learn that?" She held up a hand for me to pull her to her feet.

"A video." The second I grabbed her hand, I found myself on the ground with Instructor on top of me.

"Never let down your guard." Alice grinned and stepped aside.

Before I could react, she grabbed my hair. "Now what?"

"Ow." I tried to yank her hands away.

"No." She released me and pointed at a young woman. "You can't do the same to me."

The girl paled but stepped forward, grabbing Alice's hair from the front.

Alice put one hand over the girl's hand gripping her hair and the other on her wrist. Stepping forward and pushing down, Alice brought the girl to her knees. "Always take back control. Attack is always about being in control of you. Now pair up. Please don't hurt each other, but as I call out different scenarios, I want one of you to be the attacker. I will go around correcting the defender, then you'll switch places."

We learned knee to the groin, head butts, tossing each other over the shoulder, and taking down the assailant from every possible way they could grab us until we all lay flat on our matts trying to breathe. I glanced at Mom. "Did I hurt you?"

"I'll survive. Wait until I practice some of these moves on your father." She laughed, then raised her hand. "Instructor?"

"Yes?"

"My daughter here seems to have people shoot her a lot. Any defense against that?"

Alice blinked several times. "Run in a zigzag pattern, but if the shooter is any good, you're a goner. Hope for a physical attack."

Gee, thanks. I doubted middle-aged Margie could throw me over her shoulder.

"What kind of work do you do?" Alice stood over me. "If you were in law enforcement, you'd already know these moves."

"I own the pet store next door."

"Really? Never figured that for a dangerous job."

"I'm just lucky." I pushed painfully to my feet, then reached down to help my mother up. She pulled me down, straddled me, then wrapped her hands around my throat. "Really?"

I clamped down on her elbows and wrapped my legs around her neck. "Give?" I pushed down slightly.

"Give." She got up laughing. "This was fun, but I'll feel it in every bone in my body tomorrow."

"I think I broke something." Shar groaned and struggled to her hands and knees, then to her feet. "Alex will be proud, though. He's been on me for weeks to take this class."

"I'd forgotten they offered it." I grabbed my phone from the chair where I'd left it. "I'm hitting the showers, then taking Sheba to Brad's. See y'all tomorrow."

"Wait a minute, dear." Mom caught up to me. "I overheard something of interest as I was leaving the station after work."

"Oh?" I arched a brow.

"The robberies haven't stopped." She lowered her voice. "Another one last night. Margie must have an entire crew of thieves at her disposal. This time, they stole a rare breed of cat. The ones that look like tigers? Anyway, they didn't kill the woman but trussed her up like a turkey and took her valuables and the cat. Said the cat was worth almost three thousand dollars. Show cat."

"A Toyger?" Did Margie actually think she could sell such a noticeable breed around here? Not likely. Whoever bought it would immediately brag about acquiring such a gorgeous cat. "Did she take the papers, too?"

Mom shrugged. "They'd have the original owner's name on them. Without papers what would the cat be worth?"

"Only a couple hundred, if that much."

"Maybe she just wanted it. Of course, we're

assuming she saw the cat. Maybe the thief has a thing for felines." She shrugged again. "Not sure what we can do with this info but thought you might want to know."

"Thanks, Mom." I gave her a hug and headed to my apartment. After feeding my pets, I collected what I needed to take with me to spend the night at the penthouse. "Sorry, guys, I'd love to take you with me, but you hate car rides." I spent a few minutes with the cats and their toys, then led Sheba to the car.

As I drove, I couldn't help but wonder—why take a cat you couldn't sell for much money?

Chapter Twenty

I entered through the store, locking up behind me so the animals would follow me to the apartment. I turned the knob in the apartment door at the top of the stairs only to find it locked. What the heck? I never locked this door. Never.

Sheba tried squeezing between me and the door, releasing a soft whine. I got it. Something was wrong on the other side of that door. I stepped softly back to the store and called McIlroy. "I think someone is in my apartment."

"Where are you?"

"In the store. I came home to grab some things before heading to Brad's."

"Lock yourself in the storage room and stay put." Click.

I hid with my three fur babies and called Brad, telling him of my hiding and McIlroy coming. "I'm okay so no need for you to come running and put yourself in danger. I have Sheba with me."

"As amazing as she is, she won't stop a bullet."

"Neither would you." I leaned against the wall. "Maybe they've left. I don't hear any sounds above me."

"Don't go looking. Stay on the phone with me."

"I've nowhere else to go." I filled the time by telling him of the class I'd just taken. "You can bet I'm going to be sore tomorrow, but it was worth it."

He chuckled. "I'm glad the Waterfall Sleuths learned how to better protect themselves."

The scrape of a shoe overhead had me gasping. "Someone *is* upstairs." My heart lodged in my throat. I didn't have anything worth stealing. Whatever I did have of value was kept in the store. What could they be looking for? Since we hadn't had any clues to the identity of the thieves, then easily learned Margie's role in everything, I didn't have notes this time like I usually kept.

A knock sounded on the door. The knob turned.

I clamped my hand over my mouth to stifle a scream.

Sheba wagged her tail.

"It's me. Open up." McIlroy knocked again.

I yanked the door open. "Someone is still upstairs."

"That was me." He eyed the phone in my hand. "Say goodbye to Brad. I'll take you to his place after you look around upstairs."

I did as he said and followed him to my apartment. The place had been trashed. Again, what could someone have been looking for? "I don't get it. We know it's Margie. I'm not a rich woman." I righted a lamp. "Scare tactics? Nothing could be

169

worse than the hunt through the woods."

Glancing around, he said, "She might be looking for where you might go."

"The address to the penthouse? I need you to help me put the cats in their carriers. I'm not leaving any behind." I pulled the carriers from the closet and packed the animals' food.

McIlroy looked as if I'd asked him to brush their teeth. "Do they all have to go in the squad car?"

"Unless you want to carry them on foot." I frowned. "Your back seat is plastic. What's the big deal?"

"Won't they howl?"

"Yes." Seriously, what was his problem?

He sighed. "I hate that sound."

"You can handle a few minutes of listening to them complain." I grabbed Trashcan and handed him to the detective. "Into the carrier, please." I then fetched Sharkbait from behind the sofa and put him safely away. "Let me grab a change of clothes. I'll clean this up tomorrow."

"I'll send Murphy to case the scene first. Wait until after work tomorrow before returning." Carrier in hand, he led the way down the outside stairs to his car.

Both cats yowled the full fifteen minutes it took to reach the penthouse. Pain etched McIlroy's face. I stared out the passenger window to hide a grin.

"Most women would be silent from fright rather than laughing," he said. "Your apartment was broken into, remember?"

"Old hat." I faced him. "I never took you for

such a softie. It isn't the noise the cats make; it's the fact they're unhappy that concerns you."

"So what?" He kept his gaze on the road and turned into the parking garage of the apartments.

Brad waited by the elevator and rushed forward to help me with the animals. "Thank you for bringing her."

"Not a problem. With her luck, she'd have been run off the road again." He handed one of the carriers to Brad, then climbed back into his car.

"McIlroy thinks Margie was hunting for your address," I said, following Brad to the penthouse.

"We've good security here."

"It was breached before."

"By a dirty cop and a person pretending to be a waiter. There's no way she'll get through. I've already warned the day and the night doormen no one comes up here without being escorted by me. Not even you."

"Why?" I tilted my head.

"Because if Margie gets her hands on you, what better place to hole up than here? If a gun is being held to your head, you'd not hesitate to bring her here."

"Only if I knew you were gone."

He grinned. "Always thinking of the safety of others instead of yourself."

"Oh, I think about that, too."

The next morning, he took me and the dogs to the store. "Barney has a training session at four, and I'll be on a conference call. Do you mind?"

"Not at all." I leaned over for a goodbye kiss. "Heather will be relieved to only watch the store for an hour instead of all day while I chase crooks."

"I'll see you at dinner. How does Italian sound?"

"You cooking?"

He nodded. "I'll bring your morning coffee in a few minutes."

"Sounds perfect." I exited the car, taking the two dogs with me. The cats I'd pick up later.

As I unlocked the door, Shar and Heather arrived for work. "How was your day of rest?" I asked Heather.

"Wonderful. David took the day off, too, and we took Robbie to that indoor trampoline place. After hearing about the self-defense class from Shar, I should have joined you. Nowadays, those skills are definitely needed." She didn't add "around you," but I got the message.

"Every bone in my body aches."

"Tell me about it," Shar said. "I fell asleep on the sofa last night during the news. Which was interesting by the way."

"Oh?" I held the door open.

"A house fire on 105. Little dump of a place, home of a man who served time in prison for robbery." She tapped her temple. "My brain went immediately to the possibility that Margie is cleaning up loose ends."

I rolled my eyes. "Just because the guy stole before doesn't mean he did again."

"Arson is suspected."

"Again, doesn't mean Margie is involved." I sat in my office chair. "I need to leave a little before four today."

"Not a problem," Heather said, putting Barney in the pen. "We only have a couple of boarders and three dogs in daycare. Easy day."

"Speak for yourself. I've a full day of groomings, plus a meeting with the man who's going to make the inside of the van exactly as I want it. He should be here any minute. Said the van would be up and running in a week." Shar hurried to the grooming room.

I told Heather about my apartment being broken into. "So, I'm at Brad's for a few nights."

"Difficult living in such luxury." She grinned.

"Sure is." I laughed. "I never thought I'd get used to it, but it's definitely a second home to me."

"Someday it might be your only home."

I shook my head. "I'd like a house in the country on an acreage."

"What about the upstairs apartment?"

"I could rent it and keep the door leading to the store locked. Nothing to worry about for a while. I'm in no hurry." I had the best of both worlds—a handsome man, independence, and no pressure to set a date. Something I would do when the sleuthing bug had been exterminated.

A man with a leather toolbelt around his waist entered the store and asked for Shar. "I'm here to take measurements."

I knocked on the glass. Shar turned off the water and put the wet shih tzu back in its cage, holding up a finger that she'd be there in a minute.

"Nice dog." He motioned to the barking Barney. "I've got my eye out for a beagle pup."

"Sorry. This one isn't for sale. I can put your

name and number down if I hear of any."

"Thanks." He handed me a business card, and I wrote what he wanted on the back. Mrs. Bridges might know of someone with puppies.

Shar led the man to the alley, returning a few minutes later. "I gave him a drawing of what I want. Holler if he needs me." She rushed back to the grooming room.

I hoped the man did finish in a week. Shar covered a lot of ground with the mobile grooming and preferred going house to house rather than have owners bring their pets here. The owners preferred it, too.

At three-thirty, I loaded up Barney, leaving a sad Sheba behind so Barney wouldn't be distracted, and set off to Mrs. Bridges'. Barney had become better at walking on a leash, improved at barking, but once he had his nose to something, he couldn't be deterred. That's what Brad wanted to work on.

"He's growing fast." Mrs. Bridges scratched behind the dog's ears. "How'd the collar work?"

"Pretty good, for the most part." I explained what Brad wanted.

"Let's take the collar off and try enticing him with treats." She set the collar and remote on a patio table and led Barney to a fresh patch of dirt.

He immediately sent dirt flying.

"No," Mrs. Bridges said firmly. "Come, Barney." He ignored her. "Hm. Stubborn little guy." She replaced the collar and tried calling him again. When he didn't respond, she pressed the vibrate button, increasing the velocity until he came to her. When he did, she pulled a treat from her pocket, repeating the exercise until he came without being buzzed.

She then removed the collar again. "You try." She handed me a fistful of treats. "Has he found anymore buried treasure?"

"How did you know about that?" I widened my eyes.

"Margie Flamell told me just the other day that he found her deceased husband's watch. She didn't seem to care much for this little guy. I had the impression she's the one who dropped him on your doorstep."

"She is. Any idea where she's gone?"

"No. Said something about her grandfather's cabin and taking a vacation."

"She doesn't have any pets, does she?"

"No, came by inquiring about pit bulls for sale. I told her I didn't know of any."

"Any beagles?"

"I'll check and send you a text. Think I know of someone with a litter soon."

"Excuse me." I sent a quick call to McIlroy who said he'd have Murphy look into possible properties. He was headed to the hospital to pick up Rickson who had been released to go home. I also asked about the fire on 105. He said it wasn't connected because the fire came from the meth lab operated there, and that Shar needed to stop speculating.

I spent the rest of the hour rewarding Barney for coming when I called. Hopefully, he'd do the same for Brad. "Come on, boy."

He responded with vicious barking, his gaze on

something behind me. He only behaved this way for one person. I turned and stared into the stern face of Margie before my gaze dropped to the gun in her hand.

Chapter Twenty-one

"Mrs. Bridges, please step into your cellar. I have no beef with you." Margie motioned her weapon to the storm cellar a few feet from the house. "I'll lock you in and let someone know where you are. Take that stupid beagle with you."

With a frightened glance my way, she scooped Barney into her arms and rushed down the storm cellar steps.

I took a deep breath and squared my shoulders. "You going to shoot me here?"

"Don't be ridiculous. My car is out front. Get in the driver's seat. I have someone who will drive your vehicle. Toss me the keys."

I dug them from my pocket and threw them over her head. "Oops. Bad throw."

Her face darkened. "Get them, and stop playing around."

Maybe I shouldn't provoke her. I'd go along with her commands and keep my eye out for an

177

opportunity to escape.

I dug the keys out of the grass on my way to a silver sedan where a large man in denim overalls waited. After handing him the keys, I slid into the driver's seat. Margie's keys dangled from the ignition. I thought about trying to speed away, but she moved fast for a middle-aged woman and climbed into the backseat, messing up my second plan of slamming on the brakes at sixty miles per hour and sending her through the front windshield. With a sigh, I started the car. "Where to?"

"Just drive. I'll tell you when and where to turn."

"Killing me won't stop the police from going after you." I pulled away from the front of the house. "Why so fixated on me?"

"You're a nuisance. When you and the other two were helping me, y'all weren't too much trouble. Then you'd be busy tracking down thieves. But, you shut down the dog ring, found Joe, and ruined my easy way of making money. This is simple revenge, nothing more."

I glanced in the rearview mirror to see my car following. "Why the pit bulls?"

"Because I thought you'd have that monster dog of yours with you. Thought I'd need the protection." She laughed. "Imagine my joy when you were with the rowdy beagle."

She wanted to hurt my Sheba. I slammed on the brakes. "Maybe you should have considered the shelter."

She banged against the back seat.

My vehicle rammed into the back of us.

Margie hit me with the gun. "Stupid woman."

"Foot slipped." I rubbed the back of my head and pressed the accelerator, frowning at my vain attempt to disarm her. They hadn't taught this in self-defense class.

My head hurt where she'd hit me but not nearly as much as realizing I'd left my cell phone in my car. I glimpsed in the rearview mirror again to see the driver toss something out the window. Didn't take much to guess what he'd thrown. How would Brad find me?

If I wasn't so used to being in such a predicament, I'd have cried. As it was, I'd have to free myself. Problem was, I had no clue how. Big problem.

"Take the next exit, then turn right," Margie said. "Three miles down the road at the yellow mailbox, take another right up the hill."

If she got me to the cabin, I'd be a goner. I took the exit but sped past the mailbox. "That mailbox?"

"Idiot. Turn around."

"The ditches are too deep. I'll have to wait until a space shows up." Which I hoped would be a house or a place of business. Somewhere I could cry out for help.

"I know what you're doing, and it's no use. There's no one around for miles."

"What about a place to turn around?"

"Nope. Not for a while, but we have a full tank of gas and nowhere to be. There is a lake, though. We could end things there."

I'd take my chances at the cabin. McIlroy might find the address before I met my end. I stuck my

CYNTHIA HICKEY

arm out the window and motioned for the man behind us to back up. When he did, I inched forward and backward across the road until I faced the right direction. Let him turn himself around.

I turned at the yellow mailbox and drove to a rather nice cottage built to resemble a log cabin from the good ole days. "Nice place."

"Grandpa built it with his own hands."

"Yet you're going to sully the place by killing me here."

"No, that would be my nephew. The one driving your car." She laughed and opened her door. "Let's go."

Taking a deep breath in a vain attempt to steady my nerves, I followed. Inside, a gorgeous Toyger cat wrapped around my legs. "Why'd you steal him?"

"Johnny thought I might like him. Sit in that chair." She waved to a straight-backed chair with a wicker seat that had seen better days. In fact, the outside of the cabin was in better shape than the inside.

Faded, delipidated furniture that had to have been left behind by her grandfather filled the place. I sat in the chair where Margie used a dishtowel to tie my hands behind my back. I stifled a grin. Better than a zip tie. The woman wasn't as smart as she thought.

"Where are you going to skulk off to while your nephew does the dirty deed?"

"I've hired a private jet to take me to Europe where I'll start all over." Margie grinned. "Just me and my new cat." She patted Johnny on the shoulder on her way out. "Wait until dark, then finish her and dispose of the body down the well." Without a backward glance, she picked up the cat and left, slamming the door behind her.

Johnny pulled out a knife and started whittling next to the unused rock fireplace. He didn't spare me a glance as if I were nothing more than a bug that needed squashing.

How could some people kill with so little remorse?

"So, how are you going to do it?" I asked. If I had to sit silent for three more hours until dark, I'd go insane.

He glanced up, surprise in his eyes as if he'd forgotten why we were there. "Haven't decided whether to make it fast or have some fun. That's what I'm thinking about."

With the slow way he spoke, he didn't strike me as particularly bright. I hoped to use that to my advantage.

"Is your aunt paying you?"

His brow furrowed. "No."

"Well, she paid the other guys." I shrugged. "Does that seem fair to you? Just because you're a relative doesn't mean you should do her dirty work for free."

"That's right."

"Maybe you should go after her. Let her know you'll only finish the job after she pays you."

"Can't. She told me not to leave until you were dead."

"But she hasn't paid you to kill me. You should get paid first."

His frown deepened. "Let me think." He returned to whittling, the end of the stick in his hand growing sharper.

"Johnny?" I squirmed in my seat. "I need to use the restroom."

"Don't have one."

"Not even an outhouse?"

"It's outside. I'm not supposed to go outside yet."

"You'll have to go out to drop me down the well."

"After dark."

Oh, for crying out loud. I moved my hands around in the dish towel. Had the knot loosened? Maybe. If I could get free, I felt pretty certain I could win a fight with the simple-minded Johnny. I didn't want to hurt him. He didn't seem mean; he was only following orders from his aunt. Obviously, the young man didn't have a large concept of right and wrong which Margie exploited.

"That was sweet of you to give your aunt a cat. Do you have your own pet?"

"No. I can't take care of one good enough. Had a goldfish once, but it died." He kept whittling.

"Were you sad?"

He nodded, tears welling in his eyes. "Goldie was a good fish."

"Well, there will be a lot of people sad when I die. You can keep that from happening by letting me go."

He shook his head. "Margie will hit me in my head. That's what she does when I'm bad."

Oh, that woman! "You aren't bad, Johnny. See

how nice you're talking to me?"

"Yeah, Johnny is nice."

"But killing me will be very, very bad, Johnny. The police will put you in jail. Do you know what jail is? It's a place full of mean men who will hurt you."

Fear flickered across his face. "Margie told me to."

"Your aunt doesn't always do the right thing, but you can."

He cupped his head, dropping the sharpened stick. "I have to think." He lumbered outside.

With him out of sight, I worked feverishly on loosening the towel binding my wrists. At last it fell free. I jumped to my feet and searched for a way out other than the front door. The one-room cabin offered only a window. The similarity to the cabin part of the escape room didn't escape me.

I sprinted for the window and fumbled for the latch.

Johnny stepped back inside and roared when he spotted me . He darted forward and grabbed a fistful of my hair, yanking me back. I stomped on his foot and placed one hand on his and the other on his wrist, pushing with all my might.

He cried out, his grip loosening. I punched upward on his nose, then kneed his groin. Finally, free, I grabbed his whittled stick before making a beeline for the front door and to my car. No keys. I whirled and raced for the trees.

"You aren't being nice!" Johnny thundered after me.

"Sorry, but I cannot let you kill me." I ran in the

direction of the road. I hadn't spotted a single car while driving on it but held onto hope one would show up.

The trees weren't as thick here as the haunted forest was, providing less coverage for my flight. When I became winded, I hunkered behind a bush, gripping my wooden weapon. After a short time, I ventured out, listening for Johnny's heavy step.

He sang the song kids did while playing hide-n-go-seek. The sound chilled my blood. What I had assumed was the mind of a simple man might very well be the one of an insane killer.

I scooted into the shadows as he passed, making as much noise as a bull in full charge. Once past, I resumed my desperate flight toward the road.

"I see you!" He gave chase, his long legs eating up the distance. His arms wrapped around my waist and lifted me off my feet.

I slammed my head back. His nose crunched. Stars swam before my eyes. I jabbed his arm with the stick.

He yelled and dropped me.

"Sorry." I took off like a shot, knowing that once the surprise of my fight wore off, he'd be on my heels again.

"You're going to get me in trouble with Margie."

"You should have gone and asked her for money," I said, increasing my speed past what I thought possible. If the poor fool had left like I'd asked, I'd have escaped without him having to get hurt.

I still didn't think him mean, despite his not

giving up on the chase. Poor man was afraid of what his aunt would do to him if I escaped. Still, I wouldn't make it easy for him. If I had my way, I'd have already hitched a ride and left him far behind.

Not seeing a car, I darted to the trees on the other side of the road. I'd have to follow it back to town but would need the trees for coverage.

Johnny stepped into the moonlight on the other side and waved.

Chapter Twenty-two

Finally, the welcome sound of an engine reached my ears. Taking my chances, I stepped into the road and held out my thumb as a semi roared over the hill.

Johnny pumped his arm up and down to get the driver to honk. I rolled my eyes and climbed into the cab when the truck stopped. This time, I waved as the truck moved forward.

"Where to?" The driver asked.

"The police station."

He cut me a quick glance. "That big guy back there bothering you? Did your car break down?"

"Something like that." I leaned my head against the window, relieved my dash to freedom had come to an end. The truck stopped in front of the station, waking me up. "You're a lifesaver, sir. Thank you."

"Take care of yourself, little lady. You look as if you've had a time of it." Bless his heart, he waited until I was safely inside the station before pulling away.

A handcuffed Margie stared wide-eyed from where she sat in a chair against the wall. "Where's Johnny?"

"Where I left him at the side of the road." I doubled up my fist and gave her a strong right hook before McIlroy rushed over and pulled me away. "You should be ashamed using that poor man the way you do."

"Settle down, Ashford." McIlroy led me to the conference room. "Sit. I'll call Brad, then you can fill me in on what happened."

"How did you find her?"

"We'll talk once I have her booked. I promise. You know where the water and coffee are. Help yourself, but stay away from Flamell."

I scrunched up my face, headed to the restroom, and stared into the mirror. I did look a sight. Ratted hair, face bruised, and dirty. Every bone in my body ached from the self-defense class and from using what I'd learned for real. There would have been no other way for me to escape a man of Johnny's size if I hadn't taken that class.

I wet some paper towels and washed up the best I could, using my fingers as a comb. Not much improvement, but hopefully I wouldn't frighten Brad when he arrived.

As I left the restroom, McIlroy led Margie to a holding room. I made a move as to lunge at her, laughing as she flinched. "If only you knew what I would do to you if we were alone. You aren't so tough without your gun, are you, Margie?"

"Ashford," the detective warned. "Back to the

conference room."

Instead, I turned as Brad called my name. He rushed toward me, gathering me into his arms. "You're safe."

I nodded, pressing my forehead against his chest. "The man she left me with didn't really want to hurt me."

Mom and Dad joined in a group hug. "When Brad said your phone wasn't working…"

"I'm okay."

We headed for the conference room and took our seats to wait for the detective. "The man Margie controlled threw my phone out the window."

"We found it." Brad gripped my hand. "I've already ordered you a new one."

"If someone would have told me years ago," Dad said, "that my baby girl would be chasing down killers, I would've told them they were out of their minds. You give me gray hairs, girl."

"You had gray hair before you were forty," Mom said. "Don't blame that on Trinity."

"Okay." McIlroy entered and took his seat. "After locating your phone by going to the last known location, we lay in wait for Margie. Not many other routes she could've taken, and it paid off. We laid a strip across the road and stopped her. She gave up without a fight. Guess she knew she was no match for three gunned lawmen."

"Three?" I tilted my head.

He nodded. "Rickson insisted on coming after finding out you were missing."

"Can someone go get my car? They'll find Johnny there. Don't hurt him. He doesn't know any better." I gave them directions the best I could. "I'm sure he's still looking for me. He won't stop until Margie tells him to." I explained the man's mental state.

"How did you escape?"

"Margie tied my hands with a dishtowel. Guess she isn't used to taking hostages. I climbed out the window, Johnny and I fought, and once I broke free, I ran, hitching a ride on a semi-truck."

"You fought a full-grown man and won?" McIlroy's brows almost touched his hairline.

"Thanks to the self-defense class and sheer fear." I grinned. "Margie told him to kill me and throw my body down a well."

Brad's grip on my hand tightened. "Why did it take him so long?"

"He was trying to figure out how. I'm not sure he's ever killed anyone before. I almost talked him out of it until he saw me untied and charged. Can I go home now? I'm tired."

The detective nodded. "I know where to find you if I have more questions, although the facts are pretty clear. I'll head out and see if I can find this Johnny fellow. The judge will listen to your story and put him in a state hospital rather than prison."

"What happened to the toyger cat? Did Margie have it with her?"

McIlroy nodded. "It was a bit shaken up, but fine and is back with its owner."

Brad stood and helped me to my feet. "What you need now is lots of sleep. Don't worry about work tomorrow. The other two can handle things."

For once I didn't argue.

Back at the penthouse, I curled up with my fur babies on Brad's king-size guest bed and didn't wake until nine a.m. The aroma of brewing coffee filled the place, luring me like a bear to honey.

I found Brad sitting at the kitchen table, coffee in one hand and a newspaper in the other. He glanced up and smiled. "Good morning."

"Good morning." I kissed him and headed for the coffeemaker. "I didn't know anyone read the real paper anymore."

"I prefer the feel of newsprint when reading the news. Top story is about you bringing down Margie Flamell and putting an end to the burglaries plaguing this town."

I shuddered. "Last time I made the front page, someone came after me."

"Sweetheart, you manage to get into trouble whether you make the paper or not."

True. I shrugged and filled my cup. "Think how boring your life was before you met me."

He laughed. "Although I now live with my heart in my throat, I wouldn't change a thing."

"Most men wouldn't be this supportive." I smiled over the rim of my cup as I sat across from him.

"Well, I'm not most men. I know a good thing when I see it, and you, darlin', are the best. I do ask one favor though."

"Name it."

"That you wait a few months between crime solving to give this heart a break."

The End

Check out Unwanted Christmas Guest by scanning
this QR code.

Dear Reader,

If you enjoyed *Four-Legged Suspect*, please leave a review on Amazon and Goodreads. Reviews are the lifeblood of authors.

Thank you and God Bless,

Cynthia Hickey

Website at www.cynthiahickey.com

Multi-published and Amazon and ECPA Best-Selling author Cynthia Hickey has sold close to a million copies of her works since 2013. She has taught a Continuing Education class at the 2015 American Christian Fiction Writers conference, several small ACFW chapters and RWA chapters, and small writer retreats. She and her husband run the small press, Winged Publications, which includes some of the CBA's best well-known authors. She lives in Arizona and Arkansas, becoming a snowbird, with her husband and one dog. She has ten grandchildren who keep her busy and tell everyone they know that "Nana is a writer".

Connect with me on FaceBook
Twitter
Sign up for my newsletter and receive a free short story
www.cynthiahickey.com

Follow me on Amazon
And Bookbub
Enjoy other books by Cynthia Hickey

The Tail Waggin' Mysteries
Cat-Eyed Witness
The Dog Who Found a Body
Troublesome Twosome

Brothers Steele
Sharp as Steele
Carved in Steele
Forged in Steele
Brothers Steele (All three in one)

The Brothers of Copper Pass
Wyatt's Warrant
Dirk's Defense
Stetson's Secret
Houston's Hope
Dallas's Dare
Seth's Sacrifice
Malcolm's Misunderstanding

Fantasy
Fate of the Faes
Shayna
Deema
Kasdeya

Time Travel
The Portal

Tiny House Mysteries
No Small Caper
Caper Goes Missing
Caper Finds a Clue
Caper's Dark Adventure
A Strange Game for Caper
Caper Steals Christmas
Caper Finds a Treasure

Wife for Hire – Private Investigators
Saving Sarah
Lesson for Lacey
Mission for Meghan
Long Way for Lainie
Aimed at Amy
Wife for Hire (all five in one)

A Hollywood Murder
Killer Pose, book 1
Killer Snapshot, book 2
Shoot to Kill, book 3
Kodak Kill Shot, book 4
To Snap a Killer
Hollywood Murder Mysteries

Shady Acres Mysteries
Beware the Orchids, book 1
Path to Nowhere
Poison Foliage
Poinsettia Madness
Deadly Greenhouse Gases
Vine Entrapment

CLEAN BUT GRITTY Romantic Suspense

Highland Springs

Murder Live
Say Bye to Mommy
To Breathe Again
Highland Springs Murders (all 3 in one)

Colors of Evil Series

Shades of Crimson
Coral Shadows

The Pretty Must Die Series

Ripped in Red, book 1
Pierced in Pink, book 2
Wounded in White, book 3

Worthy, The Complete Story

Lisa Paxton Mystery Series

Eenie Meenie Miny Mo
Jack Be Nimble
Hickory Dickory Dock

Secrets of Misty Hollow

Hearts of Courage
A Heart of Valor
The Game
Suspicious Minds
After the Storm
Local Betrayal

Overcoming Evil series
Mistaken Assassin
Captured Innocence
Mountain of Fear
Exposure at Sea
A Secret to Die for
Collision Course
Romantic Suspense of 5 books in 1

INSPIRATIONAL

Nosy Neighbor Series
Anything For A Mystery, Book 1
A Killer Plot, Book 2
Skin Care Can Be Murder, Book 3
Death By Baking, Book 4

Jogging Is Bad For Your Health, Book 5
Poison Bubbles, Book 6
A Good Party Can Kill You, Book 7 (Final)
Nosy Neighbor collection

Christmas with Stormi Nelson

The Summer Meadows Series
Fudge-Laced Felonies, Book 1
Candy-Coated Secrets, Book 2
Chocolate-Covered Crime, Book 3
Maui Macadamia Madness, Book 4
All four novels in one collection

The River Valley Mystery Series
Deadly Neighbors, Book 1
Advance Notice, Book 2
The Librarian's Last Chapter, Book 3
All three novels in one collection

Historical cozy
Hazel's Quest

Historical Romances
Runaway Sue
Taming the Sheriff
Sweet Apple Blossom
A Doctor's Agreement
A Lady Maid's Honor
A Touch of Sugar
Love Over Par
Heart of the Emerald
A Sketch of Gold
Her Lonely Heart

Finding Love the Harvey Girl Way
Cooking With Love
Guiding With Love
Serving With Love
Warring With Love
All 4 in 1

A Wild Horse Pass Novel
They Call Her Mrs. Sheriff, book 1 (A Western
Romance)

Finding Love in Disaster
The Rancher's Dilemma
The Teacher's Rescue
The Soldier's Redemption

Woman of courage Series

A Love For Delicious
Ruth's Redemption
Charity's Gold Rush
Mountain Redemption
Woman of Courage series (all four books)

Short Story Westerns
Desert Rose
Desert Lilly
Desert Belle
Desert Daisy
Flowers of the Desert 4 in 1

Contemporary

Romance in Paradise
Maui Magic

Sunset Kisses
Deep Sea Love
3 in 1

Finding a Way Home
Service of Love
Hillbilly Cinderella
Unraveling Love
I'd Rather Kiss My Horse

Christmas
Dear Jillian
Romancing the Fabulous Cooper Brothers
Handcarved Christmas
The Payback Bride
Curtain Calls and Christmas Wishes
Christmas Gold
A Christmas Stamp
Snowflake Kisses
Merry's Secret Santa
A Christmas Deception

The Red Hat's Club (Contemporary novellas)

Finally
Suddenly
Surprisingly
The Red Hat's Club 3 – in 1

Short Story

One Hour (A short story thriller)
Whisper Sweet Nothings (a Valentine short romance)

Made in the USA
Monee, IL
03 December 2022

19441802R00115